# The Fair
# of Phenloris

## The Portents of Doom

# Therese Grant

*Auntie Babs, enjoy the read.*

*Love and Kisses to you.*

*Teri*

*L Grant   7/7/16*

BRIGHTON PUBLISHING LLC
435 N. HARRIS DRIVE
MESA, AZ 85203

# THE FAIRY CLAN
## OF PHENLORIS
### THE PORTENTS OF DOOM

## THERESE GRANT

BRIGHTON PUBLISHING LLC
435 N. HARRIS DRIVE
MESA, AZ 85203
WWW.BRIGHTONPUBLISHING.COM

COPYRIGHT © 2016
ISBN 13: 978-1-62183-336-9
ISBN 10: 1-62183-336-4

PRINTED IN THE UNITED STATES OF AMERICA

## First Edition

COVER DESIGN: TOM RODRIGUEZ

# Dedication

*To my publisher, Kathie McGuire.*

Y ou are an inspiration, whom I have had the privilege to work with and an honor to know. As my imagination runs wild with ideas, it is your help and gentle encouragement that keeps me enthusiastic about writing. You are a permanent part of who I am and who I have become, and I am truly humbled to call you my friend.

LAND NO LONGER REMEMBERED

# Character's Phonetic Pronunciations Key and Description

**Adwyn:** (Add-win)—Fairy Caretaker of the Clan of Oneth.

**Aleese:** (Al-ease)—Fairy Caretaker of the Clan of Coremerick.

**Alwyn:** (Al-win)—Elf Craftsman of Heartmoreland at Newry.

**Arrgoniea:** (Air-go-knee-a)—Far-away land.

**Caewun:** (Care-won)—Fairy Caretaker of the Clan of Dolbatheryn.

**Carouselling:** (Karo-sell-ing)—Far-away land.

**Cauluden:** (Call-loo-den)—Great Fey King of the Fairy Clan of Insgoud.

**Darrius:** (Dare-e-us)—Elf of Heartmorland at Newry.

**Denbighorro:** (Den-big-harrow)—Elvin Settlement at Newry.

**Farnesse:** (Far-niece)—Fairy of the Clan of Llandier.

**Fiona:** (Fee-o-na)—Fairy Caretaker of the Clan of Karapalis.

**Fitzhuwlyn:** (Fits-hue-lynn)—Castle in the Southern region at Northland.

**Fralynne:** (Fray-linn)—Elvin Queen of Denbighorro at Newry.

**Glenwyn:** (Glen-win)—Fairy Caretaker of the Clan of Coremerick.

iii

**Halcort:** (Hall-court)—Great Dear King.

**Jahvier:** (Ha-vie-air)—Fey Guard of the Clan of Phenloris.

**Kalouise:** (Caw-louise)—Elvin Princess of Denbighorro at Newry.

**Karas:** (Care-us)—Elvin Prince of Denbighorro at Newry.

**Kharry:** (Carry)—Fey King of the Clan of Phenloris.

**Laqenchem:** (La-kwen-chem)—Elvin Settlement at Newry.

**Makluthines:** (Mac-loo-thin-ess)—Far-away land.

**Mawrthlyn:** (Marth-linn)—Wizard and twin brother of Merddlyn.

**Meirionwen:** (Me-ree-on-when)—Great Diamond Fairy of the Clan of Phenloris.

**Mirrorme:** (Meir-o-me)—Land Mermaid of Phenloris.

**Nestlyn:** (Nest-lin)—Elvin Settlement at Newry.

**Polnairs:** (Poll-nair-us)—Mountain Retreat near Newry.

**Rheead:** (Ree-add)—Otherland.

**Selphon:** (Sell-fon)—Elvin King of Denbighorro at Newry.

**Strenicious:** (Stren-is-she-oos)—Far-away land.

**Twaitshun:** (Tha-weight-shun)—Far-away land.

**Wenlik:** (When-lick)—Far-away land.

# Prologue

Long ago, in a land no longer remembered, there was a legend told to fairies about magical Crystal Butterflies that sought food and shelter during their migration over the many fairylands.

Meirionwen, Great Diamond Fairy, wife of King Kharry, and mother of their young daughter, Glenlillian, was the most powerful of all the fairies. Because of this, many fairy clans and the Great Wizard, Merddlyn, sought her out often. Her moments alone were few and far between and her duties were many.

On the day of the Spring Equinox, a long trial began that tore at the heart of the assembled. This trial revealed the treachery of a well-loved fey guard. His misuse of magic, spying, and continued heated arguments with another fey guard ended in tragedy. The court came to its final decision and ordered Meirionwen to encase him in crystal forever. Although crystal Encasement was not a common practice, it could be called upon in extreme circumstances. This action always left her depleted of energy and filled her with great sadness.

"Kharry, I need to be alone now. I was not expecting this trial to go on as long as it did, and I am troubled by what the inquest uncovered. Please just let me be," Meirionwen sighed.

"Meiri, my promised sweet, I know you stood up for Brownthorn and did not expect that he had committed the unthinkable. You believed him as much as the rest of us, but the facts in this case came forward and the truth, as hard as it is to swallow, has shown him to be guilty of taking the life of another. I have never read nor been told of fey guards at such odds with one another. Jahvier will be missed by all of us, and justice has been served." Kharry, woodland guard, fey king, and father lowered his eyes.

Meirionwen responded in a near whisper. "My great wish is that I will never be called to do this again. Crystal Encasement is a death sentence, Kharry, and we have lost not one, but two fey guards," she said with a quiver in her voice.

Hugging his beloved, Kharry whispered, "Go, take your cleansing walk and say hello to your little piggy friend for me."

Meirionwen went to her secret place where she could glide and walk among the large willow trees that often spoke to her when she would escape her duties and seek solace. One very old willow in particular was extremely fond of Meirionwen and often wrapped its long, flowing branches around her like a hug. The affection the old willow showed Meirionwen never ceased to amaze her. On occasion, Meirionwen would fall asleep at the base of her tree while holding on to several of its branches.

She felt safe and secure when it lowered its branches to cover her like a blanket.

The tree understood Meirionwen's sorrow and decided to help take her mind off her troubles by telling the fairy about a cave that held a great treasure.

Knowing she could not resist the chance to go exploring, the information filled her imagination and quenched her desires of becoming a great fairy adventurer. Throwing caution to the wind, Meirionwen entered the cave and made fairy history.

"A torch, a torch, I call, come forth."

The floating torch came as called and followed Meirionwen into the cave. Her pet guinea pig, Wallaford, led the way.

"Are you sure a treasure hides here, Wallaford? Torch, come closer," Meirionwen said.

Wallaford spoke in low tones, and his beautiful voice bounced around the cave walls echoing in repetitive sound. After long moments passed, he stopped and looked up at the floating fairy queen. With a quiet gaze he did not move from the spot.

"Torch, rise high so that I may see."

The area of the cave where they stood illuminated before them, and Meirionwen gasped in wonder. She floated forward, lowered herself to the ground, and knelt before a large crystal chest.

"What do you think is in here, Wallaford? Should I open it?"

The sound of his yes bounced around them once again, and Meirionwen laughed at his enthusiasm.

With shaking hands, she slowly opened the box. A scrolled parchment was the first thing they looked upon. Gently, Meirionwen reached for the scroll. Lifting it up and out of the chest, Meirionwen placed it on her lap. She took a steadying breath and then carefully unrolled it.

The ancient writing was in fairy script, and her eyes feasted upon the words.

*To the finder of this magical box, beware to follow all instructions. Think hard before you act, and be dutiful to the responsibilities that lay before you. Keep detailed records of your actions and the actions of the others chosen by you forthwith. Be mindful of what you uncover, and pledge yourself to all within this box. Do not touch the sleeping treasures until you are certain and without doubt agree to be caretaker. Read the second scroll after your pledged commitment.*

"Oh my goodness, Wallaford, I do not know if I should do this. What say you?" His excitement had Meirionwen laughing so hard she started to hiccup.

"All right, here goes." After clearing her throat, she spoke in a loud voice. "I, Meirionwen, Diamond Fairy, queen, wife, mother, and member of the Fairy Clan of Phenloris, do solemnly pledge my devotion, time, and intellect to whatever is within this crystal case. I also pledge to take seriously the appointment of others to promise and pledge themselves as caretakers to all within this box." Nodding her satisfaction of her words, Meirionwen unrolled the second scroll and read the words out loud to Wallaford.

*A secret place must be the planting,*

*one keeper shall be chosen.*

*Those of each clan must speak the chanting,*

*as seeds and cocoons are unfrozen.*

*When in bloom, seeds feed the multitudes of butterflies of crystal*

*and in their wake leave their magic cocoons with plenitudes of songs celestial.*

*Twelve hundred moons pass with each cycle,*

*seeds planted four crescent moons before flight.*

*Seven flowers to nourish these graceful creatures,*

*showing them the way in the darkest of nights.*

*Do not take lightly these duties before you, for great is the task at hand.*

*Once they start, they must not stop for their grace to encompass your lands.*

*Portents of doom, disasters, and vanishing*

*come from the neglect of these treasures.*

*Sorrow like an ocean wave over hearts that will have no measure.*

Her breath caught in her throat, and Meirionwen felt tightness upon her chest. After she rolled up the list of instructions and set it next to the other scroll, she reached out with shaking hands and lifted out a smaller crystal box. Lying within this ornate box were thousands of crystal seeds that sparkled in a brilliant array of colors like many gems with the aid of the fiery torch.

"I am not sure what these are, Wallaford, but they look like flower seeds."

Closing the lid, she set it aside and looked inside the large crystal chest once again. Well packed inside the chest lay an abundance of hay that nestled and protected the treasures within.

"Look, Wallaford, these are butterfly cocoons. Hundreds of crystal butterfly cocoons," Meirionwen said. Wallaford walked closer and sniffed with great interest.

Gently, the fairy queen lifted a cocoon to the light of the torch and clearly beheld the sleeping butterfly. With a careful hand, she returned the cocoon to its resting place.

"Look, another parchment."

Meirionwen unrolled the parchment and read, once again, out loud.

*Sing the song of birthing and butterflies will come forth.*

*Place them in a hidden garden with tops upright, they must point north.*

*When they empty, unwind each cocoon,*

*as they have now become an endless thread.*

*Weave them into a cloak of magic; they protect the body, arms, face, and head.*

*No drowning, no burning, a light in the darkness, the cloak grows with the wearer.*

*Float in comfort with invisible ease; our gift to each cloak bearer.*

Meirionwen smiled at Wallaford and spoke her last words before leaving the cave.

"I must plan a trip to all the clans and declare Gilthew law so that I may bring my request to all assembled. This will help me save time and prevent telling this grand story over and over again. Are you up to traveling with me to each clan, Wallaford?"

He danced in circles and squealed with great enthusiasm in response to Meirionwen's words.

"I will begin with our clan first. I hope I am not being too presumptuous in expecting a positive response from everyone. I believe a fairy prayer is in order before we leave this cave. We shall pray first in thanksgiving that such a wonderful treasure has been revealed, pray secondly for hope that these treasures will be accepted by each clan, and, thirdly, we shall pray for the successful planting and blooming of the crystal flowers as well as a successful awakening of these first butterflies of crystal."

Patting the ground next to her, Meirionwen spoke with great sincerity. "Come, sit by me, Wallaford, and let us hope that all that has been revealed to us on this day will be accomplished."

Meirionwen began her prayer in fairy song, and Wallaford sang along in his own melodic tone. Their beautiful voices carried along the cave walls and out into the meadow of willows and beyond.

When the chanting prayer ended, Meirionwen read the last scroll, the ancient scroll of direction and warning.

These precise instructions were to be followed to the letter, and the responsibility of the finder was mentioned yet again. The scroll continued on with instructions on how to prepare the soil for planting, the special mixture added to wellspring water for nourishment, the planting schedule, and the reminder to sing the fairy birthing song to awaken the first of the butterflies.

Meirionwen repacked the crystal chest, and she and Wallaford left the cave. Before heading home, Meirionwen hugged her willow tree.

Meirionwen was overwhelmed with joy that all were in agreement to welcome the butterflies. And she was just as pleased with the final choices of the fairy caretakers.

"I cannot thank all of you adequately enough for agreeing to take on such a heavy responsibility. Being caretakers of the Crystal Butterflies is an enormous task and, as you all know by now, a very serious one. Once the ceremony of distribution and instructions begins, there is no turning back. So if anyone here wishes to relinquish their agreement and promise, please do so now. You will not be thought of harshly or belittled in anyway. But I do ask that if you have an alternate fairy in mind that you please have her come forth now, as we cannot begin until we have seven representatives present."

Not one of the assembled alternates came forward, and Meirionwen smiled. She was very pleased with the volunteers who hovered before her.

"I will begin by calling each fairy forward while the others assembled chant our thanksgiving song."

At her nod, the singing began, signaling the start of the ceremony. One at a time they were called to come forth. Meirionwen handed each fairy a lovely wooden box that had their names inscribed upon its lid in lavish script. Inside each box were the all-important instructions hand copied six times by Meirionwen, the crystal seeds, cocoons, and a blank parchment scroll for taking notes tied with red ribbon.

"Adwyn, from the Clan of Oneth."

"Glenwyn, from the Clan of Inisgoud."

"Aleese, from the Clan of Coremerick."

"Fiona, from the Clan of Karapalis."

"Olive, from the Clan of Llanider."

Caerwun, from the Clan of Dolbatheryn."

And I, Meirionwen, from the Clan of Phenloris."

A sigh of relief escaped from Meirionwen's lips, and she smiled brightly. The alternates played music on their instruments. The woodwind flute, piccolo, harp, and drum played many a merry tune. Great enjoyment was had by all as the rest of the ceremonious celebration continued on with food, drink, and plenty of hearty conversation. All that was said and done that day was properly recorded in each fairy's Introduction Ledger.

"Oh, how beautifully you have decorated your Introduction Ledger, Caerwun. I see you used your favorite colors from the purple mountain heather."

"Thank you, Fiona. May I see your ledger?"

"Certainly."

They glided together in friendly conversation, and both knew it was a momentous day.

And so the ancient scroll of direction and warning was read out loud by Meirionwen. A reminder for all to take great care of their responsibilities before the ceremony ended and they all returned to their homes.

Each caretaker prepared detailed records of the planting in their own personal journals.

The first entries logged the expected butterfly's arrival as they joined the newest awakened group, as well as the route taken when departing from one secret garden until their arrival at the next.

Seven full moons later, the chosen caretakers of each clan made the long journey to the Fairy Clan of Oneth where they held the most lavish of ceremonies. With great honor they wore their newly made cloaks woven from the threads of their own cocoons as they welcomed the butterflies for the last time. It was the butterflies' final stop before crossing the large Eastern Ocean where it meets the Lembath Sea. With lavish enthusiasm, pomp and circumstance, they would say goodbye to the beautiful and wondrous butterflies until their expected return flight twelve hundred full moons later. And so began the tradition of the care and feeding of the Crystal Butterflies.

## Part Three

### Flight of the Crystal Butterflies

# Chapter One

Only fairies with the special gift of horticulture would become the caretakers of a secret garden. There they would plant the magic crystal flower seeds at night with the aid of the soft glow of a crescent moon. One such fairy, from the Clan of Phenloris, known as Green Fairy, possessed this knowledge.

Now was the time for the second planting, and Green Fairy took this job very seriously. However, something was wrong when she visited the specially prepared garden for the tenth time in one passing of a full moon.

Green Fairy dug frantically in the soil of the hidden garden.

"No, no, no, where are you? Please, please, let me find you." Expelling the breath she held, Green Fairy gently removed one of the crystal seeds of the Cyclamen. Lifting it to the sun, its multitude of colors sparkled in a brilliant array that reminded Green Fairy of a rainbow, but she could not see the expected roots attached to this hybrid seed.

I

With great care she placed it back into the richly tilled, magically prepared soil bed next to the other Cyclamen seeds and gently covered it, finishing the task with a quiet fairy prayer. She could only surmise with great sadness that the multitude of daffodil, paper white, orchid, tulip, hyacinth, and sunflower seeds were in the same condition.

These seven varieties of crystal flowers were the only source of food for the Crystal Butterflies, who she knew from a dream her sister White Fairy revealed were on their way to the Fairy Clan of Phenloris's land; the first stop in their long journey to feed and rest. Still on her knees, she spoke to the soil.

"I cannot understand why you have not bloomed as of yet. Three full moons have come and gone, and still I have yet to gaze upon the expected multitude and variety of flowers. Why have I come across nothing? How is this possible?"

Green Fairy sat in the soil and put her head in her hands. Closing her eyes, she sought answers that would not come. Peering out of the hidden garden, Green Fairy made sure she was not seen or followed on her way to her favorite meadow to have a quiet moment to think before heading home.

It was an odd feeling for Green Fairy to be roaming the forest meadows and fields without her eight sisters' constant chatter in her ears. Their excitement was uncontrollable when their mother, Kim Gold Fairy, gave her approval for each fairy's sleepover at several neighboring fairy clans.

Green Fairy was more concerned about tilling the soil in preparation for the planting of the crystal seeds than a silly fairy sleepover. Her own excitement came when Blue Fairy told her they would all be away until the next half moon. Her smile could not be contained when she thought of truly being alone for the first time since her birth.

Green Fairy sat among the daisies in a particularly lovely field, recalling the tale of the flight of the Crystal Butterflies.

Their grandmother, Glenlillian Crystal Fairy, began telling them the story to ease their fear of stormy nights when they were still fairy babies, and it always began with their great grandmother, Meirionwen. This tale, recited to them often, never lost its magic or became boring in the telling.

Against her grandmother's constant complaint about danger, Green Fairy stood and walked, like her mother often did, and headed in the direction of her home. Taking a shortcut through a wooded area, she was not looking forward to telling her mother about the rootless seeds or that she needed to speak with her sisters to help decide what course of action should be taken to force the growth of the crystal flowers.

Her sisters were spread far and wide over the fairylands, making everything most difficult. Smiling to herself, her excitement grew at the thought of seeing all her wonderful sisters again. For it seemed to her that much time had passed since they were together, and she realized she truly missed them.

The sound of her mother's voice echoed in the distance, and Green Fairy stopped walking. Quickly turning around, she changed her course of direction. Contemplating what she would say, Green Fairy knew there was no right or wrong way to tell her mother of the disaster in the garden.

The charred remains of the old cottage Agnes had once occupied continued to smolder. Kim Gold Fairy stood shocked

3

by this deliberate destruction. It crossed her mind that Agnes had done this herself since escaping from the prison Nothingness and two sunrises had passed before Kim was informed by Clara the guinea pig that she had indeed escaped. Mumbling to herself while she paced back and forth, she whispered, "I am packed and ready to go to Rheead with my father and Huw. They will not understand why I cannot go at this moment and will surely leave without me, but I must find Agnes."

Her mind went back in time to the incident in Agnes's cottage when Kim was forced into action. Her intent was to keep Agnes from escaping into the dark haunted forest where she could hide and seek help from the creatures that resided there. Agnes had become an angry woman and an evil witch-like demeanor had overcome her senses.

Because of her wicked ways, she was banished from King Crawford's Fitzhuwlyn Castle where she worked as a maid and second-lady-in-waiting to Queen Joyce. In her anger she had kidnaped the queen's young daughter, Princess Teri, and held her captive with the intention of using her for her own gain.

When Kim and her daughters confronted Agnes, she tried to flee her cottage. In the quickest of moments, a fireball spewed from Kim's hands and hit Agnes in her back. In one fairy moment, Agnes was blown into the prison— Nothingness.

Kim's last thought before heading out to speak with Green Fairy was that her mother, Glenlillian, was going to disown her.

"Mama," Green Fairy whispered, "who burned Agnes's cottage to the ground?"

4

Kim turned around and found her daughter standing next to her.

"Are you following me? I thought you were checking on the crystal flowers. How did you get here so quickly? How long have you been standing there?" Kim ended her words with a questioning look.

"I have been watching you for a while. I did not want to disturb you because you looked so worried."

"I am, but now that you are here, I must tell you something distressing. Do not be afraid. You need to trust me. Do you trust me, Green?"

"Yes, Mama, you know I do."

After taking a deep breath, Kim spoke. "Agnes has escaped."

Green Fairy's eyes opened wide and shock was clearly written on her face. Green Fairy's mind raced with questions of how that was possible.

Zoo Zoo Piggy the guinea pig told Green Fairy and her eight sisters of Nothingness's whereabouts long ago. It had taken a great deal of their time going back and forth to ensure that Agnes did not escape. Each of them had taken turns splitting the duty of being watchers. It was a huge undertaking as they balanced that weighty responsibility with their regular duties. The threshold to Nothingness was only visible to their mother, Kim, the sisters, and Clara Piggy, Zoo Zoo Piggy's great, great granddaughter. It was her turn to keep an eye on Agnes, and Green Fairy felt sick to her stomach because her escape may have been her fault. She was so busy with her concerns over the unproductive garden, she may have let too much time pass before her next scheduled visit to Nothingness. Kim was not aware that her fairies knew where

5

Agnes was or of their secret schedule, so Green Fairy said nothing, lest she get them all in trouble.

"I must find her, but I need some assistance," Kim continued. "I have decided to bring your sisters home early to help with the search, and this will take a bit of time to accomplish. I want you to tell your grandmother about Agnes and stay with her until I get back. Can you do this for me?"

"Yes."

When Kim rose up to go, Green Fairy stopped her with her next whispered words. "The crystal seeds will not bloom."

Kim's heart seemed to skip a beat, and she was momentarily frozen, unable to move. She closed her eyes, lowered herself back to the ground, and said a quick fairy prayer that the portents of doom were not upon them. Kim's mind went back in time, and she recalled the instructions read to her by her mother, Glenlillian Crystal Fairy. Kim's eyes filled with tears, and a pounding pain drummed in her head.

The writings did not answer the many questions that arose in conversation between the caretakers, Kim and Glenlillian. Questions like: *Who wrote the instructions? How did they know fairies would find them? Who or what placed them in that hidden cave? When did they put them there? The most important question was where did they come from in the first place? Where did they go once they left the Clan of Oneth? Finally, why in all the heavens would the seeds not bloom?*

Glenlillian was the second fairy in her immediate family chosen by the clan to pass on all the information necessary for the preparation of the second flight of the Crystal Butterflies. Green Fairy was given the privilege to ready the gardens for them because she had become a great horticulturist. Kim did not want the responsibility of keeping

6

the time calendar and journal, so she asked Glenlillian to continue on with her notations. It was an honorable and important task that needed constant updating before being handed over to Green Fairy. There she would find all the instructions necessary for a successful planting and flight.

Turning back to Green Fairy, Kim spoke once again. "Tell your grandmother everything. Take her to the garden to assess it. My hope is she can figure out what is wrong and fix it." Green Fairy did not move until Kim yelled, "Go. Now."

Insgoud was the last stop for Kim, and she tried not to think of the difficult journey back to Phenloris with her daughters in tow. Purple Fairy, Orange Fairy, and Brown Fairy were visiting their cousins at Coremerick. Pink Fairy and White Fairy were with their cousins at Karapalis, while Red Fairy and Blue Fairy were in the land of Llanider seeking a special herb. Finally, Yellow Fairy was visiting her friend, Jenna, and Jenna's family at Insgoud. It was a great surprise to them both when Jenna's mother announced that Kim Gold Fairy had arrived to take Yellow Fairy home.

"Jenna, Yellow. You must follow me to the wishing well immediately." Yellow Fairy and Jenna's eyes were wide with concern, and they followed Jenna's mother to the well. There before them hovered Kim and Yellow Fairy's sisters.

After the hugging and kissing between the eight fairy sisters ended, Yellow Fairy looked directly at White Fairy with questioning eyes and wondered if she knew what was amiss. White Fairy answered her sister with one shake of her head. It was obvious to all the sisters that White Fairy's ability to glimpse bits of the future had somehow failed her in this instance. "Mother, why have you come here?" Yellow Fairy asked with a nervousness etched in her voice. "I still have time left for my visit, and Jenna and I have yet to finish weaving the last of the gathering baskets. Is something wrong?"

Kim smiled to prevent Yellow Fairy from overreacting and simply said, "I decided to collect all of you early. You and your sisters need to come with me, for I have important news to discuss with all of you and time cannot be wasted explaining everything. Come and hover next to me. Quickly."

Kim glanced at Jenna and her mother and thanked them for their hospitality. In one fairy moment, Kim and her daughters disappeared.

"Mother, did we do something wrong?" Jenna questioned.

"No. No, of course not. I am sure Princess Kimberlyn Gold Fairy Mother has her reasons for gathering her children to come home. It is not for us to question her decisions. She is often called upon for many reasons to use her power as Gold Fairy and to assist all in this land. If she wished to offer an explanation for her sudden visit, it is her right as Gold Fairy to speak on the matter or not."

Jenna nodded her agreement and glided with her mother through the plentiful gardens of Insgoud. It was time for the collecting of the passion flowers that were ready to bloom at any moment.

Insgoud had the privilege of collecting and distributing these lovely flowers to all the clans. This unique and special flower was used often in teas to calm and bring a lift to a sad mood when mixed with other herbs. In a concentrated form, it was used as an anesthetic to numb an area around a wound. Mixed with the special tree bark of the pine, it rendered the drinker unconscious.

8

The flashing scenery swirled around Kim and her daughters as the winds blew in a tight vortex. Nearing Coremerick once again, Kim decided to stop for a quick rest in the private meadow of prayer. She needed to clear her mind and organize her thoughts before speaking to her daughters. As the motion slowed to a crawl and the shimmering mist gently covered the fairies, the vortex collapsed and all fairy feet were firmly set upon the ground. Kim smiled and spoke with a gentle voice.

"I am very sorry that I have interrupted your visits, but I have a reason for gathering all of you to come back home."

Kim went into the long explanation of all that had happened concerning Agnes and the disaster in the secret garden.

"Any questions? No?" Kim asked.

Kim's eyes opened wide, for this was a moment to record in her family journal. Not one of her daughters spoke one word. Always chatty, always opinionated, they never refrained from speaking their minds. It was a temporary moment, Kim knew. But it was still a significant moment nonetheless.

With her energy slightly depleted once again, Kim still needed the strength to travel the last miles to Phenloris. Her ability to travel anywhere in a fairy moment with the added weight of her daughters did not come without its consequences. Kim was well aware of the side effects she would suffer when they finally returned.

Her girls sat down in a close circle on a soft patch of grass and quietly whispered to one another in their private, made up, language—a language they formed in their minds before they could actually speak.

A soft smile came upon Kim's face at the memory of her strong-willed daughters insisting on being called by their favorite colors. "Best and favorite color in the whole world," they had each informed her. So there they sat, speaking to each other once again in whispers, laughing softly, and always touching in loving gestures of affection were Orange Fairy, Red Fairy, Purple Fairy, Blue Fairy, White Fairy, Pink Fairy, Brown Fairy, and Yellow Fairy. Kim snapped out of her thoughts and decided to get moving again, but her girls suddenly stopped talking.

Kim looked in their direction. Standing just inside the meadow of prayer was a large stag. He spotted Kim and slowly walked toward her. With a finger to her lips, Kim instructed her girls to be silent. Not taking her eyes from his, she glided to meet this most handsome of creatures.

Kim lowered herself to the ground, curtsied, and bowed her head in a sign of great respect.

"Will you walk with me, Kim? I must tell you of an incident my great-great-grandchildren witnessed two evenings past, and it is most distressing."

"Yes, I will walk with you Your Majesty."

He was Halcort, king of the deer and very old. From the look of him, he clearly had been in many battles. Men continued to hunt him for sport but were not aware of just who they sought for an amusing and exciting kill. His death would be the greatest of tragedies, with a sorrow echoing through the ages and going on until time itself stopped. "I was taking my evening walk near my home when two of my great-great-grandchildren came bounding upon me. They had the scent of smoke on them and rushed their words of explanation for their sudden appearance. Apparently they had come upon three elves in the process of setting a fire upon a cottage. As my greats hid themselves behind a thick wall of foliage they continued to observe the group, but were too far away to understand the words of chanting as the elves set the place ablaze. A moment later there was an explosion of such force my grands were thrown several yards away. Their description of the elves was vague when I questioned them, but there was something familiar in their description about one of the elves." Pausing a moment in thought,

Halcort ended his statement with a question.

"Do you know these elves, Kim?"

"I believe you have described Egwin, Your Majesty. The elf you called 'my elf,' those many years ago. But I do not know the others. I cannot for the life of me understand why they burned down that cottage. I promise you that I will look into this matter and find the answers."

His nod of agreement told Kim he was satisfied, and in two swift movements he was gone.

Kim stood still thinking on King Halcort's words until she felt her girls take hold of her hands. Half-laughing she said, "At least I know who burned down Agnes's cottage."

As she gathered her girls around her for the last time, Kim focused for home.

# Chapter Two

lenlillian was bending down, inspecting one of the unproductive seeds. As she used the sleeve of her gown to wipe away moisture on her face from the unexpected rain, a blast of wind nearly knocked her and Green Fairy to the other side of the empty garden.

Hanging on to a giant oak branch, Glenlillian and Green Fairy waited for the wind to stop. With her focus once again on the garden, Glenlillian spoke her words with care.

"I am getting a very bad feeling about all of this. It is as if something wants to deliberately destroy every plant, tree, bush, and flower."

"I agree, Grandmother. I think we should go for now and try to figure this all out when we get home. We are running out of time, and I am afraid for us, the butterflies, and all the other clans," Green Fairy said with a whimper.

As tears slowly slipped down her face, Glenlillian grabbed Green Fairy in a bear hug and started humming the fairy birthing song.

In one flash of a moment, Kim and the rest of her daughters hovered on the far side of the garden. Moments later, Kim fell to the ground unconscious.

"Orange, fetch my medicine bag and bring it to me quickly," Glenlillian said. "Purple, I need you to start a fire and please stop this rain. The rest of you, circle your mother and use our language to speak the prayer of healing." The fairy sisters began to chant *Siarawch y weddi o iacha'u* over and over again.

With the water heated to her satisfaction, Glenlillian emptied the pouch of sage, honeysuckle, lemon moss, daisy stems, and dried porcha into the clay pot she kept in her medicine bag for emergencies.

As she slowly stirred the concoction until it thickened slightly, Glenlillian listened to her grandfairies chanting. White Fairy sat with her mother's head on her lap, quietly whispering the ancient healing words.

With the liquid cooled and poured into a small cup, Glenlillian spoke quietly to the fairy sisters. It was important to keep them calm and their minds off their obvious worry. She smiled, and while she began her tale of how she had come upon a most unusual recipe, she put the healing tea to her daughter's lips, coaxing her to drink.

"I was in the Night Garden of Rarities where the elusive Porcha Plant was ready to spring forth its one and only blooms of the season. I was chosen to be the collector of those large, fragrant flowers and stood at the ready for the action to take place.

"My large net was lying on the ground, and I tied two of its ends securely together. I commanded the net to rise up slightly, and with the other two ends tightly curled around my left and right hand, I rose to level the net.

"Like corn that pops in a blistering sun, the blooms flew off their stems in various directions, and it took all of my skill to catch every flower. If they hit the ground, they would be useless as a healing ingredient."

Glenlillian smiled at her grandfairies, who were enthralled by the tale. In the quiet of her mind, Glenlillian traveled to her garden and recalled a most surprising happening.

"Here in this garden's darkest of evenings, I felt the greatest of peace. This garden is filled with a large variety of flowers, herbs, and important weeds. It also houses the rare and elusive Suddeth Spider.

"Her web is gently collected and stored for stitching up the open wounds of elves and fairies. Elves are highly allergic to the closing cloth once used on Sir Jahaziel so many years ago. In rare cases it can cause convulsions when applied to a female elf."

Glenlillian looked directly at Red Fairy and said, "Red, be sure to remember this."

Red Fairy simply nodded, and then Glenlillian continued her tale.

"The blooms from the Porcha Plant are the last flowers added in the healing tea for curing lung infections, and the ingredient is added to a thickened paste that is slathered on the healing cloth for closing wounds.

"After binding the net ends with morning glory twine, I hoisted it up and tied it to the largest branch of a willow tree. There they waited for the sun to do its magic and start the drying process."

Glenlillian looked lovingly at her daughter, Kim, and knew the healing tea was doing its job. With mischief sparkling in her eyes, she looked at her grandfairies and spoke once again.

"Would you like to hear the tale of my meeting with the great elfin king, Selphon, and his wife, Queen Fralynne?"

All the fairies nodded their heads and waited for the tale to begin. Brown Fairy leaned in closer to be sure she could hear every word.

"I was on a three-sun-rising venture and had gone as far as Polnairs Retreat when I heard the sound of crying. Not wanting to disturb whomever was obviously there to be alone with their sorrow, I was not expecting to see the female elf in labor."

Glenlillian's mind recalled every moment of the encounter.

*Fralynne bent over once again, and breathing quickly, she could not stop her moaning. Without shame, she let her tears flow freely, for she knew something was very wrong. She had been laboring, on and off, for nearly a full sunrise, and the baby within her was unable to exit. This was her first child, and she and her husband had fought just hours before her laboring began. Harsh words were said to her about being lax in her duties.*

*He had no heart when it came to her suffering. Her inability to move quickly, due to her great size, had him in a near rage. He belittled her every time she tried to eat a little something to keep up her strength, and her tears continued as she recalled his harsh words.*

15

*"All you do is laze around and eat. Can you not go about your duties and stop all this self-indulgence? Elfin women have been having babies for eons and would not conceive of ever speaking of a difficulty or problem while carrying. Why do you complain so?"*

*When Fralynne began to cry again, her husband, King Selphon, walked away in disgust.*

*Glenlillian went to her immediately and spoke in a soft caring voice so as to not startle the elf.*

*"I am very sorry to have disturbed your private moment, but I see you are having difficulty bringing this little one into the world. My name is Glenlillian of the Clan Phenloris, and I am a healer. Please allow me to assist you."*

*"Yes, thank you, Glenlillian of the Clan Phenloris. I am Fralynne, queen to King Selphon of Denbighorro. I fear this baby does not want to come forth and grows weak from the trying. If you can help us, it would be most appreciated."*

*"It so happens I have my healing sack filled with herbs. Please sit on this soft area and rest your head against this oak tree. I will start a fire quickly."*

*As Glenlillian began a conversation with Fralynne, she became angry when she mentioned her troubles with her husband, the king.*

*"Hush, now. No reason to go back to the unpleasant. Here—drink this tea. It will relax you and the baby. Then if you will allow me to take a peek, I should know what the problem is."*

*The observance of cleanliness was an obsession with Glenlillain. It was a natural motion for her to wash her hands twice before starting any task. As soon as she realized*

*Fralynne was going to sleep, she bent down and took a peek with her next contraction.*

*"Fralynne, there is a grand surprise in here." Glenlillian smiled brightly.*

*With a panting breath, she answered, "What do you mean a surprise?"*

*"I see two babies in there and they are hugging each other. When your next contraction comes, I should be able to unwind their arms."*

*Fralynne burst into tears, and Glenlillian quickly soothed her with kind, sweet words once again.*

*"It is a good thing that I am a fairy. I have small hands, but they are strong hands and have served me well."*

*Slowly and with great care, Glenlillian was able to unwind the arms of the twins, and the first baby popped out with great speed. She caught her just in time; else she would have hit the ground hard.*

*As she wrapped the little bundle in her cloak, the bonding set, and they became part of each other forever. The second baby, a boy, took his sweet time. Once he came forth, he seemed to try looking at everything around him. As he joined his sister in Glenlillian's cloak, an unheard of second bonding set, because they were twins.*

*Fralynne spoke in a whispered voice. "Look, Glenlillian, he holds on to your finger and does not wish to let go. He is strong, is he not?"*

*"Yes, they are both strong and healthy, and I have been blessed to be a part of this wonder. I believe this is not a chance meeting between us."*

17

Fralynne nodded her head in agreement, and she held her two babies with such tenderness it brought tears to Glenlillian's eyes.

Satisfied that all was well, Glenlillian took a few moments to coo and smile at the precious bundles. She spoke in a near whisper as to not startle the twins.

"Do you have names picked out, Fralynne?"

"Yes. Karas if it was a boy and Kalouise if it was a girl."

"Those are beautiful names and to think you get to keep them both."

Glenlillian moved from her place next to Fralynne and added kindling to boost the fire once again. Using the last of the water she'd gathered, she brewed up her healing tea and explained the tea's purpose.

"Fralynne, this tea will help you gain your strength quickly, and you should be able to leave for your home well before the setting of the sun. I will accompany you to be sure you are safely returned."

Nearing Fralynne's home, at the base of the Newry Mountains, Glenlillian announced her request.

"Please allow me to speak with your husband first, Fralynne. It is important to me." Nodding her yes, she stayed near the side entrance to her home as Glenlillian entered with caution.

"I am sorry, but who did you say you are?" the king questioned.

"I will tell you my name in a moment, however important or unimportant it may be to you; but understand me *well, King Selphon, I will hurt you. I will hurt you and make you sorry we ever met."*

This of course was a lie, but Glenlillian had to emphasize a little power behind her stern words. Although she had been recently crowned Golden Fairy at that time, which carried great power, she was quite incapable of harming anyone or anything in spite of her anger at that moment.

*"I am Glenlillian Gold Fairy, and I will not allow you to speak to your wife in the manner you have to this point. I will send fey guards here on a regular basis until I am satisfied you speak in sweet wooing words to your wife from now on. And if it is reported back to me that you have been remiss in your duties to your wife or that her feelings have been abused, I will have you carted away and imprisoned at the first tear witnessed flowing from your wife's beautiful eyes."*

The fairy sisters covered their mouths to stop the laughter trying to escape as they waited for Glenlillian to continue. They all knew the truth of those words spoken to the king. Their grandmother's sternness, as well as her stubbornness, was a thing of legend. Once she made her mind up, only fey magic could change it.

*The king's fear overcame his anger, and he knew well who was hovering before him and he spoke with great sincerity.*

*"I apologize most humbly, Glenlillian Gold Fairy, for my insensitivity to my wife's condition. I am a first-time father and do not have a patient nature. But, I will practice until it bursts my heart if you will reconsider."*

*"Your words please me. Now let us bring in your wife."*

*After the king's initial shock over the twins wore off, Glenlillian spoke with careful words.*

*"This is the reason for the extra weight of your wife, and her laboring was long and difficult. You, sire, would be at this very moment mourning their deaths at graveside had I not come along when I did."*

*"I know this to be a truth, and I apologize to you, Fralynne, my beautiful wife, and to you Glenlillian Golden Fairy of the Clan Phenloris."*

*After his weeping ended, the king spoke once again.*

*"I will, from this moment on, understand better the sufferings of others and give aid whenever possible."*

*Satisfied with his sincere words, Glenlillian was very happy to stay a while to celebrate with the new parents.*

*Now drunk, it seemed, with happiness, relief, and celebration, King Celphon insisted on payment. Naturally, Glenlillian declined. However, she did not wish to cause yet another argument and gave in, telling the king the only thing she was interested in were recipes.*

*He gave her his prized secret recipe he called Gwynness and explained its preparation for a most magnificent and tasty brew.*

*King Selphon kept his word and grew in grace and strength. Stories of his kindness and generosity spread throughout the lands, and he continued to be sought out often for his intellect and opinions.*

As Kim slowly began to come around from her faint, Glenlillian bent down and kissed her daughter's forehead and spoke once again of King Selphon.

"King Selphon and Great Fey King, Cauluden of the Fairy Clan of Insgoud, were great friends. When Selphon told Cauluden the tale of the birth of his twins, I was called before King Cauluden and questioned. I can tell you I was truly nervous. I tried to recall all the harsh words I had said to King Selphon, but I could not. Then to my great embarrassment, King Cauluden repeated what Selphon had told him.

Before I could defend myself, Cauluden burst out laughing. He laughed until he started coughing, and I had to slap his back to right him. Once he regained his senses, much to my surprise, he spoke these words to me.

*"Glenlillian, Gold Fairy, you have shown great strength and restraint in your dealings with my friend Selphon. He truly can be a handful to deal with once he sets his mind on something right or wrong. I have had many verbal battles with him and have won few.*

*"My fear concerning Selphon has always been his temper, quick and furious with no end in sight once he starts on a rampage. Now here you are, hovering before me without one ounce of fear when facing Selphon's temper. No. You not only stood up to him, but you somehow transformed him, calmed him, and made him see himself in a different light.*

*"It is because of you, Glenlillian, that Selphon has changed for the better. Now I am privileged to see a caring, fair, and deeply reflective elfin king. Your valorous and headstrong nature saved him, his wife Fralynne, and his children.*

*"Prepare yourself, Glenlillian. For I bestow upon you this day the great title of Crystal Fairy. I will accompany you to your clan and will personally assist with this ceremonious celebration to begin immediately upon our arrival."*

21

Glenlillian smiled at the tear-filled eyes of her grandfairies and spoke in a whispered voice. "It was at this very ceremony that King Cauluden introduced me to his son, your grandfather, Lutherian."

# Chapter Three

Agnes pulled the tiny material tightly around her neck as she sat against an old, dilapidated stone wall. Tears slipped down her face, and she wiped at them with her hands. Taking a deep breath, she tried desperately to clear her mind. She did not know her name, where she was, or where she should go, but she was in dire need of assistance.

She was horrified at the prospect of steeling the minute cloak found hanging on a branch, but she was shaking from the cold and rain, and the little garment looked as if it would offer a bit of warmth. Its tiny appearance made Agnes smile slightly, because it seemed more like a cloak made for a doll.

After Agnes donned the cloak, it suddenly began to grow until it reached the ground in billowing length with the hood falling nearly to her chin. Shocked from what had just happened, Agnes cried once again. Those tears, however, were tears of thankfulness.

The warmth from the cloak finally relieved the cold stiffness from Agnes's bones, and she stood to gain her bearings. The rain pounded harder, and she realized she was very hungry and wondered how long it had been since she had eaten.

Turning toward the sound of rustling leaves, Agnes spotted a fox peering at her. His attitude was that of a calm animal. He wagged his tail and cocked his head to show Agnes he was unafraid. Agnes slowly opened her cloak and motioned the fox to come to her. Once again she sat against the wall and carefully wrapped them in the growing cloak and hugged the little creature to her. Her last thought before falling asleep was, *I am no longer alone.*

When morning arrived, Agnes followed the fox through the forest until she became exhausted. After resting awhile, she spoke to the fox.

"I do not know where you are taking me, but I am so hungry and thirsty, I cannot think straight."

The fox nudged her once again to follow him, and Agnes reluctantly obeyed. To her great relief, the short walk revealed the open meadow before them. Around its edges were wild blackberries, strawberries, cherries, grapes, and tiny melons hiding in the shade. Snap peas, broccoli, and green peppers were damp from the recent rain, and Agnes ran to the banquet presented to her.

With her hunger satisfied, Agnes walked around the peppers and back into the forest where a tiny brook formed, curving its way toward a larger stream.

When her thirst was quenched and her hands and face washed clean of the juices that she had happily splashed on them, she bent down and hugged her friend in thanksgiving for the magnificent feast. He licked at her face and made quiet yipping sounds that made Agnes laugh.

"I must assume you understand me, and I cannot thank you enough for your help. I will trust that you know where we are going, and I will follow without complaint. However, it will be dark soon, and we must find shelter for the night. Can you do this?"

The fox ran ahead of her with great enthusiasm, and Agnes once again followed the wonderful creature she named Aidan.

They headed in the direction of the now-setting sun, and Agnes stopped a moment to look around her. She shook her head and peered down at Aidan.

"It is lovely here, but I do not recognize this place. Do you know if I have been here before?"

His only response was the wagging of his tail as he nudged her to continue. Just before sunset, Aidan discovered a large, abandoned stable and led Agnes through a side opening. Fallen trees that were quite impossible to move blocked the front entrance.

Agnes fell asleep the moment they entered the last stall, and Aidan stood watch over his charge. He knew he had little time left to deliver Agnes to Fitzhuwlyn Castle, and her safety was important to him. He was responsible for all her suffering from the moment she entered that cottage so many years ago out of curiosity and later when she returned to make it her permanent residence.

He chastised himself as his thoughts came quickly. *I do not understand how Mawrthlyn awoke. My power is much greater than his is, and I sent him to that cottage, for it was his prison. But I must get Agnes to safety before I seek my answers and question the Destroyers of Darkness. Perhaps they have answers for me. I thank the stars and heavens that I found her, but I sorrow at the loss of her memory."*

The sounds of the approaching night lulled Aidan to sleep, and he snuggled well into Agnes's side and deep into his troubling dreams.

25

Agnes awoke with a start and sat up while instinctively grabbing for her cloak. Once her eyes adjusted to the darkness, she realized she was alone.

Her mind went blank, giving her no clue as to her whereabouts, which caused a moment of panic. Agnes moved her hands around the dirt floor feeling for something recognizable. Touching the fine lengths of straw calmed her, and she recalled her journey to the old stable.

"Aidan. Where are you? Please come to me," she whispered.

The panic, hunger, and fear began to slowly return to Agnes's mind, and she fought hard to not give in to its overwhelming desire to break her.

Taking deep breaths, she slowly stood and began to walk in the direction of the opening where Aidan had taken her. Calm once again, Agnes was relieved to see the sun rising, hear the chirping of birds, the rustling of leaves from unseen critters, and the lovely smell of morning dew.

Somewhere in the far reaches of her mind, she knew these simple things had been taken away from her, and she had not witnessed the pleasures of nature for a long time. Her tears ran freely down her face, and Agnes walked ahead looking for what she did not know and for her fox.

Kim slowly sat up with the help of her children and mother. Shaking her head slightly to clear her thoughts, she asked what happened. Everyone started talking at once, and Kim had to yell for them to stop.

"One at a time, please," she said while holding her head in an attempt to relieve the pounding and throbbing pain.

Glenlillian spoke with concern etched in her voice. "I do not understand what you hoped to accomplish by moving through dimensional time with your arms full of my grandfairies, but you could have permanently harmed yourself and them."

Kim knew if she contradicted her mother, all the heavens would open up with her fury, so she kept her opinions to herself and asked for more of the healing brew.

Motioning to Red Fairy, she spoke quietly. "I need to wake up now, Red, completely awake. Do you understand?" Red Fairy's eyes were wide, and she nodded at her mother. Placing a hand on her mother's forehead, she spoke a secret chant unknown to the others and closed her eyes.

A soft mist began to cover the pair and an unfamiliar sound surrounded the garden. A moment later, Kim was hovering with Red Fairy in her arms and touching her forehead to hers. She whispered, "Well done."

Kim lowered them to the ground and a soft smile came upon her lips. "I can see you are all growing up so fast. I could not be more proud of you than I am at this moment.

"Each of you possesses unique gifts bestowed upon you at birth. These gifts are blooming to their full potential, and you must not misuse them. We have a difficult situation presented to us that needs to be resolved as quickly as possible, and I need each of you to use those gifts to help Grandmother and me right this wrong. Shall I now tell you what I know thus far?"

All the fairies nodded their heads and listened intently to Kim Gold Fairy. When Kim finished her speech, Green Fairy flitted forward and spoke quickly. "Mama, can Red Fairy wake the crystal seeds, do you think?"

27

All eyes were on Red Fairy, and Glenlillian answered the hopeful question.

"I am sorry, but Red's healing abilities are not strong enough just yet. Besides, we need more information and another assessment before we begin the task of healing."

"I think this dress is too long in the back, Mother, and too tight by far in the front." Princess Teri turned around and faced the large mirror in her mother's sewing room and smiled at her reflection.

"Nonsense, it looks beautiful. Do you like the color? I thought the near-white material was a good choice from the usual dark creams and blues used for wedding attire."

Queen Joyce hoped her daughter agreed with her and knew there would not be enough time to start sewing another wedding dress if she did not.

"No, it is lovely, and Myles will like this color for his wedding jacket I'm sure. When do you suppose we can start sewing some of these pearls onto my dress?"

"Today, if you have some time before you and Myles pack up the gifts to take to King William."

"We have already done that and decided not to go until tomorrow. I believe it wants to rain, and I do not wish to ride that distance in a deluge," Teri stated.

"I do not know how you can predict the weather like you do, and I would not have guessed in a million years it would rain today, but I do trust your instincts and..."

Queen Joyce stopped speaking when Siomara walked into the sewing room.

Nodding her head while making a quick curtsy, she announced, "Your majesty, princess, Purple Fairy is here and would like to speak with both of you."

Walking quickly to Princess Teri, Siomara spoke in a near whisper. "What a beautiful dress, princess. I so love the color. Do you think you can keep it clean before the ceremony is finished?"

All three women laughed at the comment and knew the truth of it. Princess Teri was very hard on her clothes.

"Please tell Purple to come up," the queen uttered.

Before Siomara could go below stairs to retrieve Purple Fairy, she was already hovering in the doorway of the sewing room. Princess Teri ran to meet her friend and wrapped her arms around the fairy like she would a large doll.

"I am so happy to see you again, Purple. What brings you around to us humans?" Jokingly, the princess poked a finger at the fairies tummy. Purple Fairy was very ticklish, and the princess was well acquainted with her and all her sisters.

Laughing heartily, Purple Fairy glided away from her friend and began to slowly circle her. Lifting her arms up and with wings out, she flung fairy dust at the princess. The queen and Siomara put their hands to their mouths in an effort to not cry out, but when the dust cleared, they could not help gasping in sheer wonder.

Princess Teri's dress sparkled with brilliant light from hundreds of tiny crystals. At the top of each crystal were equally small, white, and pale pink pearls permanently attached to the garment. Purple Fairy smiled a wide, lovely smile, and then spoke.

29

"It is my wedding gift to you, princess. I have not seen such a splendid gown, but I thought it needed a little something extra special, do you agree?"

All the women were touching the gown and oohing and aahing over it. Tears sparkled in Princess Teri's eyes, and she hugged her friend once again.

"How is it that you have come to us, Purple?" the queen questioned.

The fairy's smile left her face and she became serious in the telling and reason for her visit.

"I have come to warn you to be very careful when coming and going from the castle. Agnes has escaped, and all of us have been searching for her, but we have had no luck thus far. If she has entered the dark forest, it may be the reason why we cannot get a fix on her. There is no need for you to hide. Just be more careful when you are out and about." The queen held her daughter and Siomara's hand in an effort to remain calm, and the women continued to discuss the problem of Agnes's escape.

When Purple Fairy was given the difficult task of informing the queen and princess about Agnes, no one questioned Orange Fairy's decision to seek out Myles and inform him of Agnes's escape from Nothingness.

"I do not understand any of this, Orange. How could Agnes escape? And why has she not been found?" Myles spoke his words carefully to the fairy.

"We do not know how this has happened, Myles, or where she is. We have asked the creatures of the forest to keep their ears and eyes alert to her presence. Our hope is she will be found soon."

Myles nodded his head with understanding and spoke once again.

"I was just on my way to convince Christopher to come with the princess and me to Castle Mead to visit King William. He has not been feeling well, and Queen Joyce has packed up a wagon for us to take to him. Teri has decided to leave very early tomorrow because she is convinced it will rain today. To be truthful, I hope she is correct in her strange ability of weather prediction. Our crops have not been doing well, and the seeds we planted do not want to come up. Perhaps this rain will be just the thing to start their growth."

Orange Fairy hovered motionless and could not seem to breathe. Her face turned ashen white at Myles's words.

"Are you all right, Orange?" Myles touched the side of her face and moved her long, dark blonde hair over one shoulder to get a better look at her. Her large, black eyes focused on Myles, and she spoke her words very carefully.

"We seem to be having the same problem. You know Green is in charge of the wedding flowers, and she has overworked herself getting them to grow. She has complained to me that they are much smaller than they should be and have no scent to them." Orange Fairy was careful not to mention the crystal flowers since they were a fairy's concern and were to remain a secret thing.

Myles squinted his eyes and spoke with great care and love, for he and Orange Fairy had become great friends and were bonded years ago at their first touch.

By commission they had gone on many special and secret assignments on behalf of King Crawford. Orange Fairy's ability to become invisible had served them well, and it continued to surprise Myles each time she would disappear in front of his eyes.

"What are you not telling me, Orange?"

"I cannot say, Myles. Please do not ask me. It is a family matter."

"All right, I will leave it alone for now. How about coming with me to collect Christopher? You know he will be very happy to see you."

Orange Fairy's crooked smile and gleaming eyes put Myles on guard. Then she spoke with all the mischievousness a fairy possessed. "Want to race?"

"Oh no, you little cheater, get back here," Myles yelled with laughter in his voice while he ran in the direction that Orange Fairy had flown.

# Chapter Four

In the darkness of the night, within the shield of the densest forest, the Secret Society gathered for an emergency meeting.

"What do you mean a bit of the darkness escaped, Linden?" Staring across the campfire at his friend, Egwin waited for the answer.

Farian spoke first in an attempt to avoid the argument he knew would come.

"Because we had very little time to prepare, our efforts did not immediately contain the dark evil residing beneath that cottage."

Farian quickly held up his hand for silence and continued. "Our Elvin Secret Society meetings did not prepare us for such a standoff. How long has it been? Three moons since we became aware once again of this darkness so long laid to rest? Why has it decided to spew forth now? And do we know what awakened it?" Pointing to Egwin he spoke again. "You are the head of our society and keeper of the Ledger. Did you really expect it to lie dormant forever or for things to go smoothly without objection from that thing?"

"Are you quite sure it is dead, Farian?" Linden questioned.

"Yes. No. Maybe? I am not certain, Linden, but there is more bad news. That bit of oozing darkness rushed out and caused some irreversible damage in its attempt to escape, and the human residing there must have been killed as well. I saw no body, only signs that someone was living there."

"What damage?" Egwin shouted. "What human?"

The argument went on for long moments before the three elves settled into silence. As each stared into the fire, a collective sorrow settled over their minds, and the reality of the future was a daunting thing indeed. At last, Egwin quietly spoke. "Which one of us is going to tell her?"

King William was clearly embarrassed by the show of affection from his visitors. He was, however, very grateful for the medicine sent by way of Red Fairy and the much-needed gifts of furniture to replace the ones destroyed years ago after the war with King Arnault ended. King William did not have the heart or time to commission new furniture to be built, so the interior portions of Castle Mead that needed his attention were ignored. He used his time and energy repairing the huts occupied by servants, craftsmen, and weavers that were burned, some beyond repair, from the fire set by the warring king.

Sometimes working well into the night with the people, King William ignored his empty main hall, kitchen, and guest quarters, his growling stomach, and his health until he was satisfied his people were sheltered and comfortable once again.

After several years, the scant furnishings began to deteriorate. So he decided not to replace them, for he liked the openness of all the rooms. Besides, he rarely had visitors to impress, and he was as frugal with money for himself as he was with visits to other kings and lands. However, he was impressed by Jahaziel's generosity when he offered William the money he collected from the sale of King Arnault's magnificent ruby ring.

Queen Joyce, on the other hand, decided it was high time her cousin had proper furnishings. Like a long line of marching ants, servants happily brought in the gifts. Among the lot for the kitchen were cooking utensils, two high stools for the baker's table, and one large eating table with four matching chairs. For the sleeping rooms above the stairs, there were several large handmade quilts, wooden chests, and side tables. For the tall hearth room walls, there were two oversized tapestries depicting outdoor scenes that the queen, Teri, and Siomara had worked on for nearly a year. With a writing desk and chair set at a side window, four fireplace lounging chairs with matching foot stools set evenly at each side of the large hearth, along with a fireplace bench all stuffed and covered in a beautiful blue material, King William's receiving hall was once again a lovely and welcoming place to visit.

Assembled in his hall were Myles, Christopher, Princess Teri, King Crawford, and Orange Fairy, who perched comfortably on the high back of the princess's chair.

Each fought for their turn at telling outrageous tales to get King William to laugh. It was by order of Red Fairy that he should laugh heartily in order to loosen up the congestion in his chest and take his mind off the horrible tasting brew mixed for his quick recovery. Finally getting his chance to speak, King William questioned. "And where is your wife, Crawford? Could it be she is hiding from me to avoid my displeasure at being forced to drink this most disgusting brew?"

"Trust me, William, if my wife came with us that brew would have already been poured down your throat before you could scream a protest. Lucky for you she had wedding issues to discuss with the servants and could not come at this time."

Gregarious laughter issued once again, and King William coughed until tears burst from his eyes. The princess's face turned a light shade of pink, clearly embarrassed by the mention of the upcoming wedding. Myles took her hand in his, and they stared at each other for a moment. A silent understanding passed between them, and their excitement grew. Soon their future together would come to pass.

All eyes focused on the couple, and King William spoke with a sincere heart. "I cannot tell you with sufficient words just how happy I am for you and Myles, Princess. Let then my gift to you reflect my happiness."

King William bellowed for his friend and butler, John. At his entrance, the king asked him to fetch the wedding gifts. John smiled a huge smile, nodded, and then ran out of the receiving hall in haste to do his king's bidding. He was, however, extremely pleased that he would be present to see the looks on the faces of the assembled to witness their surprise. Everyone remained silent, waiting in anticipation for what would come. Then the recognizable sound of horse hooves on the stone floor echoed through the castle as John walked slowly back into the receiving hall. Centered between them, John held tightly onto the reigns of the two large, white unicorns.

A unified gasp was heard by all, and Orange Fairy flew to hover in front of King William to give him a piece of her mind. But before she could speak, the king held up a hand and spoke with rushing words. "Orange, let me tell you first how I have these unicorns in my possession before you blast me with your anger and turn me into a tree or ivy bush."

A smile came to the fairy's face, and her anger slowly receded.

"After the siege on my castle ended, and I gratefully witnessed my people rescued from that awful dark forest by you and your clan, I went on retreat to Polnairs. I wandered for months in quiet mediation contemplating the damage to my lands as well as the damage to huts, homes, and the forests within and outside of Mead's borders. The fire set by that guttersnipe, King Arnault, caused me much pain. Since then I have made it a point to visit the retreat at least twice a year.

"On a recent pilgrimage, I somehow became confused and walked further away than I had before. After a mile or two more, I came upon another forest beyond Newry that was unfamiliar to me. Naturally, I became curious and continued on. The forest that lay before me was enchanting with such splendid attire that I could not walk further, fearing it would be a dream for which I did not wish to waken. Uneasy that it could disappear before my eyes with just a blink, I continued to stare.

"I do not know how long I stood so transfixed that I did not notice the two little baby unicorns approach. They came to me without fear and began to lick my hands in a welcoming gesture. I snapped out of my reverie and saw immediately that they were short of starvation and too young to feast on the wheat, oats, and corn growing so abundantly. I took them home with the intent to help them in any way I could. I presented them to a sweet horse my late wife often rode named Meagan. She had just given birth to a stillborn foal, and she began to sorrow.

37

"With caution, I led the little ones to her. With great joy reflected in her eyes, she took to them immediately. These two treasures feasted happily and grew in strength, love, and, dare I say, knowledge.

"Now, I will tell you something fantastical you may or may not believe. Not only are they unicorns—a rare animal indeed and to my understanding never before seen by human eyes—but these two beauties can also speak the human language, and I suspect other languages as well.

"They impressed upon me that they wished to be known as Enos and Elaine. Enos is the male and Elaine the female. They have agreed to be received by you Princess, for a time, and are gladdened in the knowledge that you are to be married to a kind and generous young man. We have all come to love Myles and have the good fortune to call him a friend."

Orange Fairy nodded her approval and went back to where the princess sat. Settled once again on the back of the enormous chair, she leaned close to Princess Teri's ear and whispered, "I do not have the heart to tell King William they will soon have the ability of flight."

Kim heard her name called from beyond. It reached her mind, not her ears, which left her momentarily startled, but she recognized who called to her. It was Egwin beckoning her to meet him at the meeting meadow. It was their bonding that allowed this communication between them. Kim commanded that she not be followed and left the garden quickly to do Egwin's bidding.

Glenlillian shook her head and lifted her eyes to the sky, hoping it would calm her before she spoke. Kim was never one for lengthy discussions, but the meeting was not over as far as she was concerned. They had not yet settled on a plan of action to resolve the problem with the crystal seeds. Glenlillian and her grandfairies walked around the secret garden. As they viewed the slow withering plants and bushes, a frightening thought came to Glenlillian's mind.

*Is it possible other lands are affected by this bad luck? No, no, this is not possible. This cannot be possible.*

They left the garden in sorrow, and Glenlillian spoke to Green Fairy about coming with her for a quick visit to the Clan of Coremerick. A quick inspection of their gardens and meadows would give Glenlillian her answers.

"Grandmother, what can we do?" Pink Fairy questioned.

"Before Green and I leave for Coremerick, let us search in the Cave of Scrolls. Perhaps we can find what we need there."

"Why have you called to me? I was under the impression that we were not to see each other again, and I am settled with that decision."

Egwin turned quickly around, startled by Kim's sudden arrival, but he was determined not to allow her the satisfaction of seeing him so unsettled, thus he shouted his answer.

"Can you not announce yourself before you descend upon me?"

Kim knew instantly that something was very wrong. When the elf spoke with such harshness, it was her understanding of him that kept her thoughts quiet until he spoke again. Her stance, however, shouted volumes. With her arms crossed over her chest and one eyebrow raised, the hovering fairy looked down on the elf with one thought in mind: TOAD. His stammered apology saved him.

"Forgive me, Kim. I have much on my mind, and I will calm myself before I speak again. My frustration has more to do with my exhaustion than anything else. Let us sit quietly for a moment while I gather my thoughts."

She nodded her agreement, and they sat on a large boulder. It was made of a rare black granite stone that was located in the center of the meeting meadow. The soft humming sound of recognition the bolder emitted made Kim smile, and she gently rubbed it as if it were a bald-headed infant. Mesmerized by the fairy's rhythmic hand movements, Egwin waited patiently for her to speak first. Yet he could wait no longer and began his conversation.

"Kim. What I must tell you is not only difficult, but it is quite unbelievable."

Egwin paused a moment to see if Kim was agreeable to listen. Her soft smile told him to go on, so he took a deep breath, let it out, and spoke with great sincerity.

"Let me start at the beginning. When I was very young, my father, Richmond, recruited me into a secret society known as the Destroyers of Darkness. I, as well as two other elves, have the great responsibility to remove, imprison, or destroy the dark evils that hide in many ancient places all over our great continent. My father was chosen by the society to not only fight but to write down all that happens in the Great Ledger, whether we are successful or not in our important and, might I say, sometimes difficult, tasks. The Ledger is filled with many accounts of battles fought and won or lost, and the names of all the elves past and present are listed in the back pages of the Ledger. My name is there, as is my father's and his father before him. Seven generations of prince and knight Elves of Heartmoreland. Our homes are located just beyond the Newry Mountains."

"You are a prince and knight?" Kim questioned.

His deep laughter echoed through the meeting meadow and startled birds flew out of the surrounding trees.

"You did not know your act of kindness so many years ago not only saved my life but the lives of countless creatures and a few people along the way. Had I died in those moors so many years ago, things would be very different at this moment. I know fairies are forbidden by their parents to have contact with elves until they are adults, but you fought your fearful understanding that you could be banished from your clan and nursed me back to health regardless of your laws."

Kim's face reddened at the memory and praise being given, and she spoke with a kind voice no longer agitated from the demand for the meeting.

"What darkness does your society need to seek out and destroy? If it is here, why has it shown itself in our lands?"

"These are indeed great questions that I will try to answer, but first, may we eat a little something? I have traveled a long distance to speak with you and did not have the opportunity to eat before I left, though I did have a mind to bring food with me."

Egwin reached around the large boulder and lifted a basket onto it. Kim peeked inside and saw a feast before her, and she laughed with such gusto, Egwin could not help laughing with her. Then he told her something amazing.

Kim's eyes opened wide, and she could not speak for the longest of moments. She was clearly shocked at hearing her name had also been written in the Ledger.

# Chapter Five

Agnes's eyes feasted on the beautiful landscape that lay before her. Her joy was quickly turned to wonder as she spotted the large castle some distance away. Agnes broke into a run toward the magnificent structure, and her mind raced at the thought of sanctuary, food, and, should she hope, a hot bath.

Aidan spotted his mistress and ran alongside her with as much enthusiasm as a pet dog. He jumped, barked, and ran circles around her. No longer able to catch her breath, Agnes stopped and threw herself on the ground. Aidan licked her face and laughter broke out of Agnes with unabashed joy, and she lay on the still damp grass with her hands resting beneath her head.

As her breathing slowed, she petted her fox and spoke to him with whispered words. "Who do you suppose lives there? Do you think they are nice people? Maybe we should search for the servant's entrance. I do not wish to attract attention. What do you think, Aidan?"

The fox clearly understood Agnes and pulled the sleeve of her gown to help her stand up. Once again she was surprised at his ability to know her words. She followed Aidan until they reached the eastern entrance clearly used for servants coming and going from the large kitchen rooms.

It took a moment for Agnes's eyes to adjust to the darkness inside the huge room. Agnes followed her nose, and she found thick soup simmering in a large pot over a fire, freshly baked bread, creamy butter, and milk cooling in a dairy vat. Not waiting for permission, she quickly found a large bowl, gathered all she saw, and ate with the speed of a starving animal as she looked around waiting for someone to catch her.

Agnes ate until she thought she would burst and then searched for something to wipe off her hands and face. She was not long in her exploration when she came upon the rain barrel filled to its brim just outside the kitchen door. Clean cloths sat stacked on a table near the doorway to the entrance hall, and Agnes snatched a small one, and then slowly dipped it into the rain barrel. After wiping off her hands and face, she decided to sit a moment at a far wall where a lonely chair stood guard at the fireplace. As the dying embers glowed, they flicked a golden light about the room as the chair cast its shadow, making it appear larger than it actually was. Agnes fell into a deep sleep, and Aidan nestled himself under the chair guarding his mistress with watchful eyes.

The castle's head cook, Mrs. Maggie Winthrop, burst into an upper bailey room where Queen Joyce was sorting through several chests filled with material she had collected over the years. The door swung open with great force, bouncing shut and open again. Mrs. Winthrop caught it before it struck her in the face, and she all but hollered her distress to the queen.

"You must come to the kitchen quickly, Your Majesty, and bring a guard with you. We have trouble."

"What are you shouting about, Maggie? My ears are ringing from your tirade. Calm down and start from the beginning. We can seek out Garrick on the way to the kitchens. Tell me."

"The name we are not permitted to say is sleeping in my resting chair in the kitchen, and she has a wolf with her."

"Agnes?" The whispered name came forward, and the shock registered on the face of the queen as her eyes opened wide and the hair on the back of her neck stood up. Maggie's head was violently nodding yes to the queen's question, and the queen's reaction was quick. Grabbing Maggie by the hand, she pulled her toward the staircase leading to the lower bailey where guards gathered, ate, slept, and relaxed between training and rotating guard duty. The long enclosed spiral staircase echoed with the women's voices hollering the guard's name. "GARRICK."

"Grandmother, there is a fairy from Llandier outside who wishes to speak with you," Purple Fairy said in a whispered voice.

Glenlillian turned from her reading and handed Yellow Fairy the old scroll of planting. Its detailed account of when, where, and how to plant the large variety of vegetables, fruits, flowers, and herbs were strictly adhered to by all fairy clans. She needed more information before she and Green Fairy traveled to Coremerick for the inspection of their gardens.

"Yellow, please put this scroll back in the clay pot on the top left shelf and let me know if your sisters have found anything useful in the other scrolls that may help the crystal seeds awaken."

Glenlillian glided out the front entrance of the Cave of Scrolls with Purple Fairy following closely behind her.

"This is Melody, the herbalist of the clan," Purple Fairy said, then nodded and flew to join her sisters in the search.

"Melody, it is so good to see you again. I think the last time we spoke was at the herbalists' meeting of the clans in the gardens at Dolbatheryn over twelve moons ago, I believe. Please follow me. My home is not far from here."

Melody nodded and followed Glenlillian in silence.

"Come inside, rest yourself, and allow me to fetch you something cool to drink."

Glenlillian pointed to her old, well-used, favorite chair and continued. "How are Merith and Farnesse doing? They must be ready to fulfill their promises by now, are they not?"

Glenlillian handed Melody a cup and sat in a chair next to her.

"They have both celebrated their acceptance ceremonies and Farnese and Windom have visited the Concordia Garden three times in less than one moon. The poor dears have not been successful with a baby. I visited the garden on several occasions, and I am beside myself with worry, Glenlillian. Our clan has not had a single baby bloom in just over one passing of the moon."

Melody drank deeply of the lemon raspberry fruit drink generously offered, and her hand shook when she gave Glenlillian back the cup.

"Have you spoken to anyone about this problem, Melody?"

"Just my promised fey, and he said I was not to worry, reminding me how many times we visited the gardens before we had Merith and Farnesse."

"Yes, I am sure his memory serves him well, and he is correct in his assessment. We seem to be having a season of late bloomings everywhere, and I have found our recent rains to be inadequate for nourishing our crops. Other areas I am told have had a slight drought. I am sure this imbalance is the cause of many late bloomings, but there is time before the harvest, and I am quite certain the Concordia Gardens will bloom soon enough, Melody."

"If you would not mind, could you come back with me to take a look at our garden? Perhaps you could give it a mixture or dusting."

"Of course I will, Melody. You go ahead on home, and I will be just a few sunrises behind you. I need to gather a few things first and tell my grandfairies that I will be away visiting your clan."

"Thank you, Glenlillian, I know you have many duties as Crystal Fairy, but I feel better knowing you are going to look into this for all of us at Llandier."

Glenlillian hugged Melody, waved goodbye, and went back inside her home. Sitting in her chair once again, she closed her eyes and prayed that it was just a Concordia Garden being difficult; but in the back of her mind, she knew it was not.

Her planned trip to Coremerick was no longer necessary. She knew darkness was slowly spreading throughout the fairylands. The disaster foretold, written in the ancient scrolls, was certain to come upon them. Glenlillian decided to search for Kim in hopes that she would accompany her to Llandier and perhaps Inisgoud as well. Llandier lay well

46

beyond Karapalis and their Concordia Gardens backed up to one another. Each had a Garden of Rarities that mimicked Glenlillian's at Phenloris and many herbs were available for nourishing the ground around the Concordias. She suspected that was the reason Llandier and Karapalis were abundantly blessed with such a large contingent of feys and fairies. The gardens cross-pollinated each Concordia Garden, and not one plant from either garden failed to bloom in the birthing of a fairy or fey.

There were also herbs that especially interested Glenlillian because her Garden of Rarities did not have them. She sometimes would travel the long journey back and forth to keep an eye out for new herbs.

Brown Fairy paced in circles within the confines of the dark forest's entrance. Her mother, Kim, gave her the sad task of finding Mirrorme to inform her that Agnes had escaped. While she waited for Mirrorme to hear her words to meet, her mind went back in time to Mirrorme's first meeting with all the fairy sisters and Kim's words of explanation of who and what Mirrorme was.

*"I realize this will be your first time meeting a land mermaid, but you must not think your thoughts in a rush or all at one time. She will be confused and may even run away from us. I am not aware of any other creatures such as Meme, so I cannot compare her disposition to those of her kind. She cannot speak with oral words, only in thoughts. You must concentrate and go into your inner selves with your questions, and one at a time please. Ah, she is here. Do not mind speak until I have introduced you."*

Kim turned to her friend and with open arms she hugged Mirrorme with great affection. Mirrorme was a tall creature and normally extremely slender, but she had changed for the better as far as Kim was concerned, and she was happy with the results of her instructions to Mirrorme about changing her eating habits. After introducing her daughters, she nodded to Pink Fairy, and Pink Fairy spoke in a whisper at first then her head voice got stronger after Mirrorme smiled at her.

"We have brought you a few gifts, Meme." Mirrorme's eyes widened in surprise, and her smile didn't leave her face. When she uncovered the willow basket, her stomach growled at the sight of the cooked rabbits and squirrels along with a variety of fruits and vegetables. She thanked each fairy for their kindness and generosity. Mirrorme hugged the basket to her and spoke in her head voice.

"I thank each and every one of you and say it is perfect timing. I have yet to find food and the day is growing late. To have this already cooked for me is greatly appreciated. However, I must tell you that I have gained a great deal of weight since meeting your mother. She has made it her task to ensure I eat regularly what she calls 'balanced eating.' It took me quite some time to get use to the assortment of vegetables and fruits she added to my meals. In truth, I have done well on less meat, and I feel energized after indulging in Kim's broccoli surprise."

Mirrorme and the fairies burst out laughing at her comment, and one at a time they spoke to her of their happiness at meeting their mother's land mermaid friend. Brown Fairy stood tall and spoke to Mirrorme in her thoughts before her sisters could rush in.

*"Oh, we know well our mothers broccoli surprise, and it changes constantly. Hence the surprise before broccoli is mentioned on the menu."*

*Laughter once again broke out and Brown Fairy continued her thoughts to Mirrorme.*

*"It is a good thing, is it not, Meme, that these are small rabbits and squirrels well roasted and ready for you. Since we have brought the fruits and vegetables with us and have yet to eat ourselves, perhaps we can sit and join you in this feast."*

*Mirrorme was overwhelmed with happiness and began to cry. The fairies rushed to her side and they touched her, patted her, and hugged her. Smiling and laughing, they enjoyed the time of newfound friendship. However, it was this precise moment that Brown Fairy gave Mirrorme a long, loving, and welcoming hug. That set the permanent bond between them, and from that moment, they kept each other's company often.*

*The fairy sisters could not help themselves. Their giggles had Mirrorme laughing inside her head as well. She put on her mirrored face for them, and the fairies started pushing each other away to look at their own reflections.*

*"Wow. This is really wondrous, Meme," Orange Fairy said.*

*"My turn!" squealed Purple Fairy.*

*"Stop it, Purple. I am not done yet," Orange Fairy hollered.*

*"I want my turn, Orange. Back away. Oh? Is that what I really look like?"*

*White shoved her way in and said, "I have a little mole on my face."*

*Mirrorme was having so much fun watching their antics that she laughed until tears came to her eyes, and Kim's comment had them all laughing once again. Mirrorme was in total agreement.*

*"Oh, Meme, you have gone and done it now. I fear my darling fairies are becoming vain seeing themselves in your reflective face. Could you please bring your own face forward before it becomes impossible for Huw and me to live with them?"*

The sound of footsteps broke Brown Fairy's thoughts as Mirrorme approached. When they broke their embrace, Brown Fairy's smile faded. Alerted to her worry, Mirrorme spoke her thoughts first. *Something is wrong Brown. You must tell me straight away.* After her explanation, Mirrorme sat down hard on the ground and looked up at Brown Fairy, who immediately sat next to her and waited for the shock of her words to fade.

*How did this happen, Brown? Why has Agnes not been found? Where is she hiding? I do not wish to see her ever.*

Suddenly, Mirrorme stood, and with a look of fright upon her face, she called out to Kim. *Kim Gold Fairy, a warning of impending danger. Fly quickly!* She knew not what the danger, but danger it truly was.

Brown Fairy hovered near Mirrorme and questioned her. *What is wrong, Meme?*

*Someone hunts your mother.*

# Chapter Six

It had been seven days since the visit with King William and the unicorns. Myles and Teri used that time to prepare the stables at Fitzhuwlyn's Castle for the unicorn's arrival before they went back to fetch them. They led them down an unfrequented trail through forests and a thickly wooded area close to Fitzhuwlyn to ensure Elaine and Enos were not seen by anyone on the walk back home.

They took their time settling the pair down in their own private stable. It was a well-built structure that took Christopher several months to complete, and he was quite satisfied with the results.

The stable had six stalls and was set apart from the other stable at the opposite end of the compound. It was well hidden and built for four unique horses called Arabians. Jahaziel told them that the horses were a rare breed brought from a faraway land and were of a skittish nature. The Arabians were being held for King Crawford's purchase, and the trip to take possession of them at a North/Southland stable was soon approaching. Now with plenty of food and water available, Elaine and Enos made snorting, blowing sounds to each other and were quite happy with their surroundings. As they closed their eyes and swished their tails, they fell asleep to the soft sound of Princess Teri's humming.

Walking hand in hand, the couple spoke in whispered words. With smiles upon their faces, they headed to the front entrance of the castle.

Tugging on Myles's hand while walking backward, Princess Teri decided they should take a walk through the castle's gardens.

The king himself planted Fitzhuwlyn's garden before the princess was born and contained a large variety of flowers and herbs. A large vessel was filled with water every day for the animals happily visiting, and a stone path meandered all around from one end to the other. At the garden's farthest corner was a wooden bench for those who wished to sit and enjoy the sight before them in quiet solitude.

"Do you like your wedding coat, Myles? We took great care to be sure it did not look too fancy. I know how you are when it comes to purchasing new clothes. Everything you have is very plain," the princess said.

"That is because I work a lot with Christopher and have ruined many shirts and trousers. But yes, I truly like my wedding coat, Teri. I was quite surprised when Queen Joyce presented it to me at supper. I know my attire is somewhat lacking but there was no need to make me such a splendid coat."

Before he could continue answering more of Teri's questions about the decorations for their upcoming wedding, Myles tugged on her hand to stop her from walking further and turned her around. Princess Teri's hand quickly covered her mouth as they viewed the unbelievable sight before them. The familiar garden was no longer the boast of kingdoms but a dry wasteland of weeds and dust. Princess Teri did not even realize she was crying until Myles wiped the tears from her face with a gentle hand.

Speaking softly he said, "We need to speak with the queen. If she has seen these gardens, she will be as worried as we are. My hope is she has already sent for Kim. Perhaps the queen and Kim can figure out what has happened."

When they walked into the receiving hall, Myles and the princess heard shouting coming from the main kitchen. Moving as quickly as possible, they arrived onto a most shocking scene.

Maggie, the head cook, and Queen Joyce were yelling at Agnes, who did not move from the chair she had occupied since her arrival. Garrick was keeping his eyes on the growling fox, now standing as guard in front of Agnes with an obvious warning to not approach. The most shocking of all was the look on Agnes's face. She was afraid.

"Stop this yelling at once." Myles's voice strained over the noise. The shouting stopped and all turned toward the door where he and the princess stood motionless. A quiet bliss descended upon everyone in the kitchen for a fleeting moment and then all the yelling began again, with each one trying to explain to Myles and the princess what was going on.

"Stop yelling," Myles repeated.

While listening to the assembled trying to voice their opinions, no one noticed Princess Teri walking over to the woman and the fox. Kneeling down, she coaxed the fox to come to her. Aidan walked with cautious steps, shaking with agitation. He kept a close eye on Agnes and relaxed a bit with the soft petting from the princess.

"You poor things." Princess Teri looked up at Agnes and continued speaking in a pleasant voice. "Have you been here long? I do not understand everyone's behavior, but I am sure Myles will straighten this out."

Tears flowed down Agnes's face, so the princess took out a soft cloth from the pocket of her skirt and handed it to her. Then she asked once again, "Have you been here long?" Agnes shook her head no. "Are you lost?" Agnes nodded her head yes. "What is your name?"

"I do not know my name, where I live, or where I am supposed to be," Agnes said in a whisper. Covering her face with the cloth, Agnes sobbed quietly. That was the moment Princess Teri realized everyone had stopped yelling. The shocked looks on their faces told the princess that she needed to take control of the strange situation before it got out of hand again.

When Aidan started growling, Princess Teri immediately stood and put a protective arm around Agnes. With her other hand raised, she shouted her command.

"You will not open your mouths. You will not move from where you stand. You will not approach me or this woman. Mother, that means you too. Do I make myself clear?"

So quiet was the room, you could hear a pin drop.

"Now, we have a very strange situation presented to us. This woman who sits here does not know her name," Teri said louder than she intended, "where she comes from or where she is heading. It is obvious to me who she looks like, but I know she tells me the truth. I will not stand here and listen to all of you with your preconceived notions berate this woman, draw and quarter her, and send her to the gallows. Do not stand here and tell me you do not realize something very strange is going on here. All of our plants, flowers, and herbs are dead or dying all around us. This woman, whom we are assuming we know, is not the same woman from our past. That woman would be quite capable of causing all this

54

difficulty. But this woman who sits here clearly is not responsible for any of this."

Queen Joyce seemed to stand a little taller as she approached her daughter and Agnes. With pride and wonder, she looked at her daughter and smiled. With a newfound respect, and a little sadness, the queen and mother who just moments before had hugged the amazing woman she called daughter, bowed in a slow, respectful curtsy.

No one was aware that the fox had faded—and then vanished—except Agnes. She began to cry all the harder, and both the princess and the queen attended to her.

Speaking softly, they told her to go with the servants. Agnes did as the queen requested and followed them as they lead her away from the kitchens, past the receiving hall, and escorted her above the stairs.

"Thank you for this wonderful feast, Egwin. It was most unexpected, and I will admit it has been a while since I have eaten," Kim said.

"I know this. I could feel your hunger and prepared."

Kim looked shyly at Egwin and, speaking in a low voice, asked, "Egwin. Have you heard of any other elf and fairy bonding before?"

"Ah, I was wondering when you would ask me that question. We bonded in the moors, did we not, those long years ago?"

Her nod gave his answer.

"Yes, although it is usually a singular wonder and does not happen often between elf and fairy, I have not heard of recent bondings. However, I did record that moment between us in our ledger when I returned."

"I have also bonded with Jahaziel and wonder how this can be with fairies and humans."

Egwin waited a moment then gave her his theory. "I believe bonding takes place in moments of need or distress and sometimes curiosity. It keeps the pairs involved from second-guessing themselves in a critical moment, settling the mind of the fairy or fey at that first touch. Fairies have a kind nature and feel things more deeply than we elves do. We become as close as family once the bonding is set, but I have not heard of this taking place with humans before. Again, I believe your strong bonding with Sir Jahaziel was a singular moment because you risked everything and saved his life. It is a good thing it can only happen once with each species, otherwise we would all be attached to each other perhaps in ways we do not wish to be."

"Did you know Myles and Orange are bonded?"

"I did not, and I believe Myles will have his hands full keeping up with that one."

Their laughter ended when Linden and Farian approached.

"I am sorry for the interruption, Egwin, Kim. Farian and I need to speak with both of you."

"Sit. Kim and I have plenty of food left over. Eat and we can discuss what has brought you both here for a meeting."

Each elf took turns explaining to Kim the events that led up to the fire. As they ate and spoke, she listened.

"We came to warn you that there is movement among dark things. I do not know if we are just being cautious, but I worry, Egwin, that all is not as it should be. We have fought many battles before but something here is different. It seems to me that an unknown creature is causing this." Farian ended his words with a questioning look.

"Kim, the society became aware of this darkness, or possible creature as Farian has just stated, several years ago."

Kim gave them a sharp look and a slight anger rose in her throat. "But," Egwin said as he held up a hand, "we knew it was not fully aware but stirring and seeking something, perhaps someone to assist it. The society has been keeping a close eye on it ever since. It became a part of our routine of awareness seeking. Once we realized it had achieved consciousness and awareness, we prepared for battle."

"We knew a fire was the only thing that would destroy what laid in wait beneath that cottage, but we sought to cleanse the area as well," Linden said.

Then Farian spoke of what they all knew to be the truth. "We held our ground, spoke the ancient words of command, and as that thing rushed toward us, we set the fire. We did not expect the explosion or the damage to be so great. As the smoke began to clear, we realized we did not destroy that dark thing, only wounded it. As it quickly fled from us it released an oozing darkness that followed in its wake. Once the smoke cleared, we walked around a bit then something caught our eyes, and suddenly we realized we had all made a terrible mistake."

They looked to one another and then back to Kim, but it was Egwin who finished.

"Our mistake was not checking inside each time we came to the area to be sure the cottage had not been occupied over the years. We had to wait until the fire burned out before we could walk further inside the parameters of what was left of the cottage. That was when we discovered signs of occupation. We found minute pieces of what appeared to be clothing, books, cups, plates, and various personal items, such as the handle of a hairbrush and a shoe. The fire was so intense and the explosion so strong, it was highly unlikely that any remains would be found of the human who lived there."

Linden spoke once again, "We are truly sorry for the loss of this human, and we will try to find out who it was. Perhaps we can sift through everything again and with a bit of luck find something that remains of the human. We would like to give the poor person a proper burial."

Quiet moments passed as they thought about all that had been spoken.

All the information given to Kim was still sinking in. The origins of what they called "the oozing darkness" was frightening, and she agreed that the society was within its rights to seek out the darkness and destroy it.

Then Farian spoke in a despondent voice. "It is like the blackness in space beyond the stars, because it gives no light and only knows to consume, using anything of means to reach its goal to control and dominate. If that is not achieved, it destroys."

"I know who occupied that cottage, but she was not there when you set that fire," Kim said sadly. "Rest assured and do not trouble yourselves over this. Her name is Agnes, and I removed her from that cottage many years ago and sent her to a safe place. I am confident no one has lived there since."

"What?" they spoke in unison.

Merddlyn was no longer bound by the form of fox. Satisfied that Agnes was safe and being care for, he stood his full regal height and slipped into the darkness of the forest, unnoticed. Deep in thought, he walked silently.

*It is time I search for answers. Answers that The Elvin Secret Society may have to clear up this mess. Perhaps they have contained my brother elsewhere, if in fact he is not dead. I must find out what they know and what they did with Mawrthlyn.*

*If he has deceived everyone by allowing them to believe he is dead, this would give him the time he needs to recuperate and gather strength. May the heavens above help everyone in this land if that has become the truth in this matter. His anger will be uncontrollable, and he would seek to destroy everything and everyone involved who may have attempted to contain him once again. No one will be able to stop him once he sets his path and mind on total destruction. His wrath would ensure no one would be left alive, not even me.*

His thoughts were interrupted when he heard voices in the distance. Merddlyn headed in the direction of the sound. Silently approaching the gathering, he realized the Elvin Secret Society was in session.

Kim suddenly stood and raising herself up, she hovered silently.

"Kim, what is it?" each elf asked. The wind swirled around them and soft words that only Kim could hear gave a dire warning. Mirrorme was calling to her.

*Kim Gold Fairy, I see danger approaching you. Hear my words as the wind takes them to you. Fly!*

59

"Meme warns me. I can hear her sound in the wind and in my head. We must leave this area quickly. Egwin, if I need more information, I will return here tomorrow. Otherwise, we must end this meeting now. If you need me for whatever reason, send an eagle to me with this ring." Kim took off her bracelet ring and handed it to Egwin.

"You give me this ring? Jahaziel's ring?"

"Yes. Take care not to lose it. He would be very upset with me if you did."

As Egwin placed the ring on a finger, Kim flitted forward to leave, but a strong hand caught her and held tight. She could not breathe or speak, and the elves were yelling and rushing forward to release her from the one who had seized her.

In one motion, Merddlyn threw the elves away from him and they landed in a large pile of soft leaves many yards away. Raising a hand, he slowly moved it back and forth across Kim's face and spoke in a soft voice as he hugged her. "Sleep now, little fairy. We will speak when you have awakened."

King Crawford was frowning at his wife and daughter, who were taking turns defending and explaining Agnes's sudden appearance. After holding up his hand for quiet, he spoke slowly.

"I am not happy about what I am hearing, and I do not trust that woman. I will place guards at the door of the room you have put her in, and she will not be allowed to leave. I will also place guards around our castle and centuries upon the parapets at four-hour intervals. I will not let my guard down nor rest on my laurels."

Queen Joyce had had quite enough of her husband's kingly regal bearing and speech and nearly shouted at him.

"You have not understood my words, husband. So I will speak slowly so that you will understand my meaning. If you think to overturn my decision, I will make you the sorriest king who ever lived."

King Crawford's eyebrows rose up, and his huge smile could not be helped. His wife had stood up to him. In all the years they had been together, she had never usurped his commands. From the look on Princess Teri's face, she was as shocked as her father was. A deep silence came over the three assembled in the kitchen until the sound of their hysterical laughter echoed through the halls of the castle.

"My sweet, I will not harm Agnes. However, I am most curious as to her sudden appearance and why she does not know who she is."

"This is a most unexpected event. I must seek out Kim for assistance. I am sure she can clear this up and help us decide what to do with Agnes. In the meantime, she is to be treated as a guest here and given all afforded her as a guest in our home." Queen Joyce ended her words on a sigh.

"I will dispatch Jahaziel to go to her home. He is quick and always seeking good reasons to see Kim again," the king said with confidence.

# Chapter Seven

Princess Teri knocked on Agnes's door then entered when she said, "Come in." She was very pleased to see that Agnes had stopped crying and was standing by the open shutters. Walking to her, she spoke, "Agnes, is there anything I can get for you? Do you wish something I can fetch below stairs?" Agnes turned from the window and faced the princess.

"You call me Agnes. Is that my name?"

"Yes, you are Agnes, a former lady-in-waiting to my mother."

"Can you explain what has happened to me?"

"Let me ask first what you remember before you came here," the princess said.

"I woke with a pounding headache and realized I was in a thickly wooded area. It was raining, and I was cold and hungry. I did not remember the last time I had eaten, and I wandered around in the rain for some time. I found a cloak that covered me well and a fox came to comfort me.

"We wandered around what seemed like hours then we finally came upon a meadow that had fruits and vegetables near a glen at the meadow's border. When I finished eating my fill, the fox found a place safe enough for me to sleep as the night approached. Then I came upon this castle, and you know the rest. By the way, do you still have my cloak?"

"No, there was no cloak with you when you were discovered in the kitchens."

Agnes said nothing further and pondered what could have happened to her magic cloak.

"I do not understand, Myles. How has Agnes not only escaped but ended up at the very castle she was expelled from? And why is she being treated so kindly? If I were the king, I would throw her in a dungeon and see to it that she does not see the light of day, ever." Christopher spoke his words in a near shout.

"It is a good thing you are not the king, Christopher. If you stop shouting, I will explain all that has happened and what I know up to this moment," Myles said.

Christopher nodded and pointed to the chairs nestled next to a slow burning fire in his parents' home.

"You say your parents are away seeking new building materials?" Myles questioned.

"Yes, and they decided to stay a while to be together and look around a bit. They sent me a missive and wrote that they are at an inn owned by my father's brother, Charles, in the East of Southland. He said they have not seen one another for many years and are happy to have the free time to visit. I do hope they come home soon. I have been too busy building, checking on structures, ordering extra help, and general work that I have not had much time to sleep let alone relax and enjoy a solidly well-cooked meal."

Myles roared with laughter. "Chris, all you talk about is taking over your father's business so that he may retire to the country life. The years you spent studying with the master craftsman, Sir Carl Linquest, has given you that opportunity. Your ability to build the best homes, huts, cottages, storage, and animal sheds is well known beyond us here at Northland. Rumors have spread that you have built a new type of structure that would not move in the greatest of storms or winds. Is this true?"

Christopher gave Myles a slight nod, and Myles continued his questions.

"Is it also true that you have the knowledge and skill to fix the problems in already existing, yet unsound, structures?"

"Yes, and you can wipe that silly grin off of your face," Christopher said.

With laughter in his voice, Myles asked, "Did you seriously think you would not be busy or that I would not ask you to take a look at Allenwood Castle? You know Teri and I will be living there after the wedding, and there are places not sound inside and out."

"Okay, okay. I have a proposition for you both. I need a large office to do my work and a building to store equipment and supplies. I know the castle has several outer buildings on its property and one building in particular has a small, unoccupied cottage attached to one side and a bailey attached on the other. In exchange for allowing me to make my home at Allenwood, I will make all the changes and be onsite with my most trusted craftsman who can stay at the bailey. I can start as soon as I move a few of my things and some furniture into the cottage. Naturally, I will not charge you for my knowledge and skill." Christopher crossed his arms over his chest, stretched his legs straight out, and crossed them at the ankles as he waited for Myles to answer.

"That is a splendid idea, but there is plenty of room for all of us inside the castle. Teri and I have spoken about this many times. You will let us have our way, Christopher."

Myles could not help smiling, for he had gotten his way on two points in one day. His friend would be close by, and he and Teri would not be sleeping in a room that could potentially fall down around them.

Christopher's mind went immediately to the business of the sleeping room chamber. That would be his first priority in a long list of things needing to be done, and he would not stop until it was finished. In methodical order, he began listing in his head the supplies that he would need to get started.

The silence gave way to a cough from Myles. Breaking his train of thought, Christopher said, "Let us go back to the topic of Agnes. Start from the beginning and do not leave anything of importance out."

Kim sat up and with bleary eyes she tried to focus on the fire. She could not immediately remember what had happened or where she was until a voice spoke to her.

"Kim Gold Fairy, do not worry over what has happened. I will not harm you. Sip this tea and your mind will clear."

He handed her the tea and to her great surprise, he also handed her Jahaziel's ring. Her "Thank you" was her only utterance as she put the ring on her wrist and reluctantly sipped her tea, slowly at first and then nearly finished the rest in haste.

"This tastes wonderful. What is it?" Kim asked.

"I call it my three Cs tea. Chamomile, Camellia, and Chimbote seaweed gathered from a far off sea."

"My mother would bargain me for this recipe," she said in a near whisper.

"I will give it to her freely."

Silent moments passed. With Kim becoming more relaxed, he spoke once again. "Kim, I am Merddlyn, and I have brought you here so that we may speak in private. I am seeking the one called Meirionwen, Diamond Fairy, your grandmother and mother to Glenlillian, Crystal Fairy. Do you know where I might find her?"

Kim was so shocked by the wizard's words that she started choking on the last of her tea and coughed until tears came to her eyes. Merddlyn patted her back gently until she was able to speak again.

"My mother speaks little of her mother, and I do not know if she is alive or long gone from this world. You should ask her yourself but I warn you it is a touchy subject with her. Why do you seek Meirionwen?"

"I need her help and magic to join with mine to defeat my twin brother, Mawrthlyn. He has awakened from a long sleep that I put him in many years ago. He is very dangerous and has a dark desire to destroy humankind.

"He hates people. He believes, because of their strange notions, weapons, warring, and disregard of the laws of nature, that they will eventually destroy our entire world. When he asked me to join him in his quest to destroy humans, I realized he was quite serious in his plans, and we started fighting with one another.

"I was finally able to defeat him. While he was in a weakened state, I put him in a sleep of suspension. I opened up the ground, seeking a hidden cave I knew to be in a certain area. I threw him down into it and closed up the opening, hiding it well. It is my understanding that some years later a cottage was built over the cave and several occupants have come and gone since then.

"My brother plotted his freedom the moment he became aware and heard someone walking around in the cottage. He slowly began to awaken, and he used the occupant's curiosity to gain consciousness and strength. Moments later, he realized it was a woman. And like others before her, she began to feel the cottage had strangeness to it. The prior occupants stayed a while but eventually left. As my brother slowly became aware, his conscience ebbed and flowed like the sea leaving him weak and unable to form.

The woman decided not to live there or purchase the cottage and property like the others had not due to its strange aura; but it was too late for her when she decided to climb down the ladder to the storage room looking for who knew what before finally leaving. She found the hidden door to the inner chamber I put Mawrthlyn in. Neither of them could open the door, but he began speaking to her, and—he went against all laws of wizardry when he removed that woman's will and forced her to bend to his.

"I was just awakening myself when I heard the explosion and went in all haste to the area and cave. I saw you and your daughter in deep discussion, so I reverted to my animal self, a fox, to search for the woman whom I realized was thrown out of the safe haven, Nothingness."

Kim's eyes widened and she continued to stare open mouthed. "Your quick thinking to put her there saved her from being completely taken over by Mawrthlyn. The first time she

67

set foot in that cottage sealed her fate, and she was his to do as he pleased.

"I was quite relieved when the explosion threw my brother momentarily back down into the cave, and the fire hurt him immensely. However, he was able to slink by the Destroyers of Darkness who sought him, and he is no longer in that area. Although his wounds are great, he has managed to hide from me so that he may gather his strength once again."

Kim spoke with a heavy heart. "Her name is Agnes. The woman you speak of."

Merddlyn nodded and continued his explanation. "Yes, I heard you mention her name to your daughter," he paused, and then continued. "Because Agnes was still connected to the cottage and my brother, the explosion the elves set blew her out of Nothingness. Sadly, but thankfully, the percussion removed all of her memory, including any memory of my brother. He no longer holds sway over her.

"I felt and still feel responsible for Agnes's safety, so I led her to Fitzhuwlyn Castle and remained as her fox guardian. She is being well cared for, and the people are a kind and forgiving lot. I am pleased by their ability to set their feelings aside to assist their former maid, regardless of her past.

"However, the fey occupying the space of Nothingness was blown out as well. I had to make a quick decision about whom to follow, so I choose the woman. The fey, I believe, accompanies my brother, and they conspire and hide together. This is a dangerous situation. My brother has a fey with an empty mind to fill up with his lies and hatred."

Kim took a deep breath then said, "The fey's name is Maximillian. Now I have a clearer understanding of what has happened. Yet I must tell you that your brother damaged precious plants and vegetation in his escape, and even fairy magic cannot reverse what he has done or the portents of doom that now approach all the fairylands."

Kim put her hands to her head and began to cry over the sorrow of it all.

"Shhh, little fairy. Tell me everything about this difficulty with the flowers and plants. Leave nothing out," the wizard said.

Kim calmed herself and began the long tale of the flight of the Crystal Butterflies.

After several long, silent moments, Merddlyn spoke. "Kim, do you know of the double-healing plant?"

Her excitement showed in her eyes. "Yes, I do. Will this take care of the problem, Merddlyn?"

"I am not completely certain, but I do know it must be part of the solution to be included with whatever ritual and magic is needed to undo what has been done. I believe we are both in need of Meirionwen's help and special magic. Let me tell you about the area where I last viewed this most wonderfully rare plant."

Glenlillian was exhausted. After tending to the Concordia flowers in the Gardens of Llandier and then deciding at the last minute to check on her Garden of Rarities, the trip home took longer than she expected. Glenlillian fell asleep as soon as her head hit her hay-stuffed bed top. As she lay in the large willow wood bed, she dreamed of her father long gone from this life and tears ran down her face as she drifted deeply into the world of dreams.

*"Daughter, you must remember what I say to you here in the land of dreams. You must promise me to wake as soon as we are finished with our visit. Promise me."*

"I promise, Father," she mumbled.

*"Good. I will tell you where to locate the double-healing plant for the preparation of the brew you will need to mix to wake Meirionwen. Also, bring the ancient elixir of healing called Sassafras. Brew it ahead of time and pour it over the double-healing plant. It will start healing the plant immediately. Now, and this is most important in order to be successful in wakening Meirionwen, you must gather many others with you before you enter the cave where she sleeps.*

*"Take into the cave on Bardfey Island, Kim, all nine grand fairies, Huw, Luther, and, most importantly, Merddlyn."*

Glenlillian tossed and turned and cried in her sleep. Once again she mumbled to her father.

"Kharry, I cannot release my mother. I tried many years ago, you know this. How can I release her?"

*"Huw, fey guard and harp maker, has the answer you seek. You must convince him to reveal his abilities. The plant you seek is in the Night Garden of Rarities but it hides from you because it is angry. It thinks you are responsible for the destruction of the plant life, and it hangs on with unbelievable strength to live. You must pour your ancient elixir of healing on the plant at the moment the sun lowers and the crescent moon rises. Speak and the plant will hear and understand your words. You must get its permission to remove five leaves and only five leaves for the brew of awakening and healing. Wake now, my darling, my sweet, my daughter, least you forget what I have said. Wake."*

70

Glenlillian bolted upright and flew to her writing table. Tears ran down her face as she wrote down everything said to her that night. She vowed she would not leave out one word of her father's instructions.

It was the night of dreams, dangerous and informative. Lutherian was deep in sleep when he awoke startled. His dream had shown a violent battle with an unknown enemy. He jumped from his sleeping place and hollered for Huw, first fey guard.

"I do not understand, Luther," Huw said, breathing hard from his flight.

"We need to leave Rheead and get home as fast as we can, in all haste, Huw. There is great trouble in our land, and we have much distance to travel. I hope it is not too late. A battle begins—a terrible battle. Gather everything we have collected and pack it well aboard the ship. We leave this moment. Be sure to bind all the Sassafras we have gathered tightly together. I am not sure, but I believe this is a most important plant. Glenlillian would be furious with me if I were not careful with all the plants on that long list of hers."

Lutherian shook his head in agitation.

"The large clay pots are filled with the watered-down orange blossom clover honey and marigolds as you requested, Luther. They are being sealed with the fairy wax as we speak. We can put the Sassafras in the oak barrels and the other plants in the woven Talasi sacks," Huw finished.

Lutherian left the tent erected the night before and hollered, "Raise the sails. We leave this night."

# Chapter Eight

im's mind kept traveling back and forth from the past to the present, and she could not seem to focus on a single thought. It had been a long sleepless night for her, and she glided to a small river in search of the singular plant that sometimes hid itself among the kelp and algae before she headed home.

Kim prayed that Merddlyn was correct in his assumption that the plant could be the very thing needed to help the crystal seeds bloom. The special plant was a chameleon plant and changed its color to resemble the plants surrounding it, and it could move its position from time to time. She saw the plant once as a child and gently picked several leaves from it to bring to her mother. Glenlillian was so shocked when Kim showed her the plant leaves that she could not immediately take it from her daughter's hands and just stared at it. Finally, taking the offering gently, she set it in a clay pot to dry and spoke in a near whisper.

*"Kim, watch carefully what I do. This plant is so rare. I know of only four found in my lifetime, and you, my sweet, have found a fifth. Contained within the leaves and stems are two powerful yet separate magical ingredients capable of healing the most difficult disease when dried and added to any receipt of healing."*

Kim snapped out of her memories of the past and focused on plant searching once again.

However, after miles of more searching with no luck finding the elusive double-healing plant, she decided to find Green Fairy and tell her about the plant and let her have a go in the search. She knew her daughter's skill in horticulture led her to find many new species of plants and herbs. Could she hope Green Fairy may have already come across the elusive plant?

Her train of thought was interrupted when she felt her mother and Queen Joyce were seeking her. Kim had to decide whom to go to first.

"Kim, where have you been? I have searched everywhere for you. I must take a short journey to my favorite Garden of Rarities, and I wish for you to come with me."

"Mother, I am sorry but I cannot. I feel the need to go to Queen Joyce. Take Green, Pink, and White with you."

"Kim, come back here. I must explain…"

Before Glenlillian could blink her eyes, Kim was gone.

"How does she do that?" Glenlillian spoke out loud to no one. "I am so thankful that my grandfairies do not have their mother's peculiar gifts."

As she continued to mumble to herself, Glenlillian went in search of Green, Pink, and White Fairy.

Glenlillian burst into Kim and Huw's home, but the house was empty. Looking around, she was not surprised at the many additions that had been added since her last visit.

Dried herbs hung everywhere from the ceiling and the faint smell of heather remained despite their withered state.

Heading to the back door, she decided to check the private garden her grandfairies' father, Huw, had planted years ago.

Pink, Green, and White sat on three of the eleven handmade stools that were neatly arranged in a circle. Their hands were busy with separating weeds from the kiwi plants, and they were clearly in deep discussion.

"This is ridiculous, White," Pink Fairy uttered. "This is pointless. We pull the weeds and they grow back so fast that I cannot keep up. These poor kiwifruit are dying, and we are not helping by pulling at these strange weeds that have attached themselves to them. If this keeps up, we will all be covered in weeds, mark my words."

"Stop complaining," White Fairy replied. "I know we are not as knowledgeable as you, Green, but I cannot sit and watch these poor plants choke to death."

The fairies stood at the approach of their grandmother.

"I need you three to come with me, please."

"Yes, grandmother," they said in unison.

As Jahaziel began reading the queen's missive, Siomara quietly approached her brother then quickly snatched it from his hands.

"I have not finished reading that, young lady." Jahaziel put his hand out, but Siomara moved her head back and forth.

"You need to hear me out first, and then I will return your missive. I have been looking for you for two days now, and I can only assume you will be leaving again. You just got here, Jahaziel, and I need your help."

Jahaziel crossed his arms over his chest and waited for his sister to continue.

"Myles and Teri have decided not to wait until the end of this month to wed. Considering all that is going on with the plants and other issues, they both agreed to have a less formal wedding. The princess feels a lavish ceremony would cause undue stress, and she does not want her wedding remembered as being something burdensome. They want only friends and family to attend, and I am in agreement, Jahaziel. They want to do this next week."

"And what exactly do you think I am supposed to do?"

"I need you to find Kim. The queen wishes it so. Tell her to bring Green Fairy along. We need to speak to her about the flower arrangements."

Jahaziel burst out laughing and pointed. "Read the missive, Siomara."

Looking at the missive then back at her brother, she waved her hand and hollered, "Well. Go!"

When Jahaziel peered at Siomara, she dropped the missive and ran. Jahaziel was quick and snatched her up off her feet before she could escape outside. Laughter and screams from his tickling bounced around the great hall, and Jahaziel gave in to her pleas to stop.

Setting her back down upon her feet, he held her tight, kissed the top of her head, and spoke quiet words to his sister. "You are my heart, Siomara." He did not see the tears in her eyes or the smile on her face, but he knew they were there.

"Egwin, she has to be here somewhere. We cannot let harm come to her, for she is an integral part of our society and we cannot continue without her."

Farian's voice broke, and he sat down where they stood to catch his breath.

Egwin and Linden sat on each side of Farian. In the silence of the approaching evening, they closed their eyes and joined their wills to seek the whereabouts of Kim Gold Fairy.

"I assume you are looking for your fairy?"

Merddlyn stood in front of the elves and was prepared for their anger, but it did not come. All three elves just stared up at the wizard in stunned silence.

"Kim is well and on a quest to find a special plant. I am here to offer the society my assistance in the obliteration of this darkness we have all been inconvenienced with."

"Inconvenienced with?" Farian shouted.

All three elves stood, but Egwin held his friends back with a strong arm and spoke.

"I must apologize for my friends' anger, Merddlyn, but we are all tenderhearted when it comes to Kim."

"Yes, I see your love for her grows, and it is as it should be; especially in you, Egwin. You are bonded, and her welfare is most important to you."

"I thought you would still be on retreat, Merddlyn. My father told me of your injuries long years past, and your desire to recover led you to a secret place none know of. When did you wake?"

"And how is Richmond these days, Egwin?" The wizard did not answer the question posed to him about his awakening. They would not understand that it was by the command of Renewal that he did so.

"He is well. Thank you for your inquiry."

Farian stepped closer to Egwin.

"Are you going to properly introduce us or do we have to butt into this conversation and be rude?"

Merddlyn smiled and put out his hand to Farian. "It is a pleasure to meet you, Farian, and you Linden."

Linden nodded to the wizard but did not put out his hand for a shake.

"I grow restless and need to walk about awhile. Come with me, and I will tell you all the society needs to know and what to do to rid this land of my brother."

Merddlyn linked his fingers behind his back and walked slowly through the wooded area. The elves followed and thunder could be heard in the distance as an approaching storm echoed their mood.

"Ah, perhaps this rain will feed the poor shriveling plants and flowers. I understand from Kim that many plants suffer from my brother's wrath."

"This is news to me," Linden said.

"Myself as well," Farian piped up.

"Are the trees affected, Merddlyn?" Egwin asked.

"Not at the moment. However, eventually the trees will be affected. It is just a matter of time. If my brother is not found and placed back in suspension, his plan to remove humans from this land will become a harsh reality. This plan began the moment he escaped. A dark trail of anger oozed out from behind him and set forward the slow destruction of flowers, fruit-bearing bushes, and their foliage. The trees will wither, and the shade they provide will be removed. The sun will grow hotter, and all creatures will die from thirst and starvation along with the humans. A slow death is his plan, I fear, and there is no ounce of goodness left in him."

"Do you know where he is, Merddlyn?"

"I feel, more than know, he has left this area and has gone north, Linden."

"What does he seek north?"

"I believe he travels to the very most northern end of this land. He must do this by the cover of darkness, lest he be seen by fairies, elves, or humans. There he will be able to gather strength from the land of Oneth where much is available to heal him, as well as to increase his abilities. A well-hidden cave sits just at the edge of the Oneth River. It is a place we were told about and visited many times when we were quite young.

"Our father, Grand Wizard Nealsgould, was preparing us for instruction, the law, duty, and the heavy burden and responsibility of all wizards. The cave holds the properties of all magic. It is only viewable and accessible from the shores of Oneth. The one we call Renewal resides in the cave, and she is of an unknown origin. She does not speak of where she hails and is very protective of the cave. The opening is visible only to wizards and cannot be breached by any other creature or man."

Linden and Farian spoke in unison, "Are you saying this creature called Renewal is an ancient?"

"Yes, and although Renewal has free will to do and be as well as assist any wizard in his seeking and growing, she has always liked Mawrthlyn. I fear he will sway her somehow to reveal her origins to him. If she does that, he will acquire all of her knowledge, abilities, and the secrets she has held to herself. I tell you this in all secrecy. You cannot share this with anyone. Not even Kim. Do you understand?"

"Yes," they spoke and nodded at the same time.

"We need to leave as soon as you are able to gather provisions. We must be observant as well as diligent if we are to track down my brother and his whereabouts. You must not discuss our trip with anyone. If Kim questions you, tell her you have a family emergency and will be gone for several passings of the moon, Egwin."

"Oneth is a long journey, Merddlyn, and the society has never gone on a quest so far northwest of our own lands. You need to understand Kim's roll in all of this. Her name was entered into our ledger many years ago. She must come with us if we are to be successful in finding and containing your brother."

Egwin ended his words but his face showed his worry.

Merddlyn was not happy that Kim was destined to journey with them on the dangerous quest. Not until that very moment did he realize her presence was imperative. He did not like the thought of her being harmed or worse, but he did not question fate.

"What of our fathers?" Linded questioned.

"I will speak to them. They are still members of this society and can be told of this quest. They can reestablish themselves as active members of the Destroyers of Darkness and protect the lands here while we are gone."

Farian burst out laughing. "Oh, you have no idea what you have just proposed. Our fathers have been looking for any excuse to become active again. They are bored with their retirement and drool when reading the current entries in our journals."

"I will accompany you to your homes. I would love to see your fathers again, and I am in need of a good laugh and hearty food," Merddlyn said.

"You will get both from them, Merddlyn, mark my words," Egwin said with a chuckle.

"Sir Gauwain, how have you come to be here at Fitzhuwlyn?"

Queen Joyce held out her hands, and the knight took them both. In knightly fashion, he kissed her knuckles on both hands. He could not contain his smile.

"You look well, Your Majesty."

"I am, and you? How have you been?"

"I am well, and Mr. and Mrs. Jones said to pass along their good wishes to you, the king, and the princess. I have come seeking Sir Jahaziel. I need his assistance at Allenwood. It seems the men are once again fighting among themselves, and a cottage was burned down. The old man who lived there was injured and had to make other arrangements for shelter. I went there by order of King William to fetch his man servant, Thomas, who had been visiting his sister, and I found the disarray."

Queen Joyce placed a hand to her heart. "I am so sorry to hear this, Sir Gauwain. Jahaziel just happens to be visiting his sister, and they are walking in the gardens. When you are finished speaking with him please come and sit at the table with us. The nooning meal is being prepared, and we would love to have you as our guest."

"It would be my pleasure Your Majesty." Gauwain bowed and headed out to search for Jahaziel.

Jahaziel and Siomara were in deep discussion as they sat upon the bench in the garden.

"Are you angry that I have purchased the vast lands around our parents' home?"

"No, Jahaziel, only surprised. I thought you had given up on us returning home. I assumed that you had given our house to Uncle Sabastian. Why have you done this?"

"We need to think on our future. Although we have made our home here at Fitzhuwlyn and Allenwood, I thought some day you would wish to return and maybe have a place of your own when you are grown and married."

Siomara looked at Jahaziel with loving eyes. Her heart felt warm hearing his words of concern for her future. She knew he would never force her to marry and that purchasing the land around their old home was very thoughtful of her brother.

"I have no intention of leaving my home here at Fitzhuwlyn, Jahaziel." Before he could speak she spoke again. "I think we should keep it as a place to stay when we are traveling to North/Southland and beyond when seeking supplies and other goods. We can stay for a week or two, visit with family, and not be forced to stay with Uncle Sabastian while we are there. He is far too bossy and thinks we are still children."

Jahaziel laughed and nodded. "You have quite a good head on your shoulders, Siomara. I had not thought on that. I, for one, am glad that I will not be persuaded to stay with Uncle Sabastian when I am in the area. We can talk later about purchasing furniture and material to make it a lovely home once again. Would you like to bring your friend Sara along on one of our trips? With the exception of my room, perhaps she can help you decorate since she has a way with flowers and decorating. I am sure you ladies can bring new life back to the old place."

"I know Sara would love that. Yes, let us plan the next trip when you have time."

Sir Gauwain slowly walked toward the gardens. He was in deep thought about what he should say to Jahaziel. He did not want to seem overly concerned, but Jahaziel needed to understand the serious disarray at Allenwood required his immediate attention. Sir Gauwain was not prepared for the sight before him, and he stopped walking. He watched Jahaziel and Siomara strolling to the well, and the cracking sound from the dried dead leaves beneath their feet left him temporarily speechless. He remembered the garden being grand and the talk of villages, but it was a shocking and sad sight that lay before him.

"Jahaziel, would you give me a coin, please? I would like to make a wish."

"You are a grown woman, Siomara, and I believe this to be a waste of a good coin."

"Perhaps I could be of assistance."

As they turned to face Sir Gauwain, he reached into the pocket of his jerkin and withdrew a coin. Handing it to Siomara, he smiled but could not take his eyes from her. As he continued to smile, the sound of a cough drew his attention.

82

Jahaziel's grin and Siomara's wide eyes had Gauwain taking a step back, and he spoke a bit louder than he had intended. "What? Why are you looking at me like that?"

Siomara spoke in a rush before her brother had a chance to say something inappropriate. "Pay not one bit of attention to him, Sir Gauwain. He is muddleheaded from the lack of food and is in need of rest as well."

Sir Gauwain burst out laughing. "All right. I just happened to be taking a stroll before going in to the castle to enjoy a feast I was recently invited to partake in. I came here to seek you out, Jahaziel. I wish to discuss a matter in great need of resolving."

Jahaziel nodded. "Walk with me and tell me all, Gauwain." Siomara curtsied and excused herself.

"Before I begin my explanation of why I seek your assistance, I am wondering what has happened to this lovely garden, Jahaziel."

"Truly, I am clueless, Gauwain. Now tell me what is troubling you, quickly. I must leave here as soon as possible and seek out Kim by the queen's request."

Gauwain told Jahaziel of his discovery of the recent troubles at Allenwood.

"Is tomorrow soon enough for us to travel to Allenwood?"

"Yes, I believe it can wait until then. In the meantime, I see your sister approaching to hurry us along to the meal."

# Chapter Nine

Kim rose up at the approach of Jahaziel and smiled a truly wondrous smile.

Jahaziel returned the smile and spoke, "This bonding does come in handy, Kim, and saves me a lot of time searching for you. Once I closed my eyes and focused on your face, I had no trouble discovering where you were."

Kim floated toward Jahaziel, speaking as she came closer. "You look well, Jahaziel."

"You look tired, Kim." Gently, he took several strands of her long curled hair and brought it to his face, closed his eyes, and breathed in her scent.

Kim blushed and snatched her hair away. "Jahaziel, stop that. What if Huw were to see you sniffing at my hair?"

They both burst into laughter, and Kim floated next to Jahaziel as he walked out of the meadow and down an unfrequented path with his horse walking slowly behind him.

"I have come seeking you and Green. Queen Joyce has need of your company, and some changes are being discussed about the approaching wedding. Will you come back with me to Fitzhuwlyn and speak with the queen?"

"Of course I will. However, I was already on my way to her when I felt you were seeking me, and I turned around and headed in your direction. Green is a little busy at the moment. I doubt she will want to come with us."

Jahaziel mounted his horse, and before Kim could float ahead, he snatched her around her waist and settled her close to him. They spoke of many things on the ride back, such as things of concern, plans, Huw, and the future of their land. Jahaziel was informed of everything Kim knew, including Merddlyn, his brother, and his dastardly plans. A long moment of silence engulfed them before Jahaziel finally spoke again.

"Kim, this is incredible and disturbing information. Although I am a mere human with no special gifts to offer you, I do offer you my strength and always my friendship. I will do what I can and whatever you ask of me."

Tears welled in her eyes, and Kim could only nod, as she was overwhelmed by Jahaziel's response and his generous offer to help.

Filled with sorrow, exhaustion, and fear, Kim fell asleep in Jahaziel's familiar arms. Her last coherent thought before giving in to sleep was that she needed to find Jahaziel a wife.

"Kim, it is so good to see you once again."

Queen Joyce held out her hands as they met halfway in the receiving hall of the large hearth room that now featured two giant fireplaces. Jahaziel excused himself and went in search of Siomara. Then his stomach growled, and he thought on the last time he would have eaten. Walking through the long hallway, he bellowed his sister's name as he approached the kitchen. He was hopeful that she could pack a bit of food for him before he and Sir Gauwain left for Allenwood.

"When did you add this second fireplace, Joyce?" Kim asked. "It looks wonderful and very welcoming."

"Crawford decided to hold his meetings with his knights here in the receiving hall when the weather is cold and windy. One fireplace was not enough to keep everyone warm throughout the long winter months, and the cooks need access to this larger fireplace when guests arrive. Now they have the choice of using one for their roasting and baking and the other for warming this area. Not to mention the small fireplace in the kitchen being available as well. You must come and see this wonderful idea Crawford had built into the new fireplace."

Kim floated as Joyce walked closer to the newly built hearth and pointed.

"Although it is slightly smaller than the other, this fireplace has the capacity to bake many loaves of bread, several chickens, and whatever the cooks come up with, because Crawford had our iron smith build this wonderful, yet removable, iron stacking unit." Joyce closed one of the specially built iron doors and continued her explanation.

"When shut, these ornate doors contain the heat, allowing everything to cook faster. With the doors open, it helps add heat to this large open area. We have all been playing with it and experimenting so much that we have to schedule time with the fireplace."

Their shared laughter could not be contained. Kim spoke as she wiped at her eyes.

"I think my mother would like to be included in your baking schedule."

Joyce pointed to the comfortable chairs nestled close to the old hearth. "Let us sit awhile so we can catch up. Although I sent Jahaziel to fetch you, I am still in awe that you understand when I need to speak with you, Kim; and I am very glad you have come so quickly. Jahaziel told me you were already on your way here when he came upon you."

"It is our special gift of friendship that alerts me of your desire to speak with me. It is a handy thing, do you not agree? Besides, Jahaziel is the best person to seek me out if my presence is required here at Fitzhuwlyn. You did the right thing in requesting his assistance."

"Yes," the queen said.

After they laughed once again, the queen continued, "I am grateful for Jahaziel's help with many issues."

The queen paused a moment to gather her thoughts. Then she leaned closer to Kim and spoke.

"I have something extraordinary to tell you, Kim." Joyce took a deep breath. "Agnes was discovered sleeping in a chair in our kitchen, and she is at this very moment above stairs resting. Her tale is an extraordinary one, and she should do the telling, but I can say she would not mind me giving you some of the minor details."

Kim could not discuss what she knew with Joyce, so she put a look of surprise on her face and opened her eyes wide.

"I see you are as surprised as the rest of us."

"Yes, I am surprised, Joyce."

Kim hoped her lie would not show on her face, for she was a very poor liar.

"The poor dear cannot remember a thing before we discovered her. Naturally, and understandably, we were all yelling and discussing what was to be done with Agnes, as if she were not even present. After everyone calmed down, she was questioned. Teri, however, knew instantly something was wrong and became Agnes's protector. She harbors no ill will from the past and immediately took charge of the situation. If I did not know any better, I would suspect Teri's mind had gone as well, for she seems to like Agnes, and Agnes truly likes Teri."

Tears filled Kim's eyes as her mind wandered back in time to the birth of Princess Teri.

"The moment I saw her trying to look at me, I knew she would grow to be a wonderful woman, Joyce," Kim said.

With her eyes shining with unshed tears, Joyce smiled.

"What sweet words, Kim. A mother can never receive enough compliments about her children."

"Do you think I could speak with Agnes for a few moments?"

Kim could not tell the queen about her conversation with the wizard or the fact that Agnes would never regain those memories taken from her. Yet, Kim still needed to question Agnes to discover how much of her memory had been removed.

"That would be wonderful. However, I should tell her slowly about you. I do not think she laid eyes on fairies after her mind went. Perhaps a slow introduction would be best. Also, Teri and Myles have decided to hold a small family wedding. Since we have been having so much trouble with plants, flowers, herbs, and fruits, they decided not to stress everyone out by holding a lavish affair. I was wondering if you know why this is happening, and if you have experienced anything of a similar nature."

Kim shook her head no. She had no intention of telling the queen the real reason everything green and flowery was dying.

"Merddlyn, is it really you?"

Richmond grabbed the wizard in a bear hug and tried to lift him off his feet. Their laughter echoed out into the night as Egwin, Farian, and Linden smiled at the sight of the elder elf and wizard.

"I am sorry about the loss of your sight, Richmond. Had I known I would not have gone on retreat. I should have searched for Meirionwen straight away to heal you."

"Do you know where she is, Merddlyn?" Egwin walked forward and questioned.

"Not at the moment. However, her presence is greatly needed to fix more than one disaster," the wizard replied.

"I do not understand," Farian said. Before he could continue, Linden asked the question for him.

"What disasters? We know of only one disaster."

Merddlyn looked out of the receiving room window of Richmond's home and paused a moment to watch the rising sun's approach. Quietly whispering ancient words of thanksgiving for another day of life, Merddlyn turned back to the assembled and answered the question.

"It seems my brother, Mawrthlyn, has taken a fey of Phenloris by the name of Maximillian as his personal slave. He was thrown out of Nothingness along with a human woman named Agnes and is brain-emptied. No memory of who he was remains. This gives Mawrthlyn an empty vessel to fill with his lies."

Before Merddlyn could go further, Richmond spoke.

"I need to understand what is going on here." Turning to the sound of mumbling, Richmond continued, "Merddlyn, please start at the beginning. I need to understand what is happening here."

Merddlyn spoke with a heavy heart and told his friend everything that had occurred since the escape of Mawrthlyn, Maximillian, and Agnes. Then he disappeared before their eyes. All assembled spoke in one voice and hollered, "Merddlyn, come back here!"

"Luther!" Glenlillian hollered.

Embracing Glenlillian, King Lutherian held her tightly and waited until his heart stopped pounding before he spoke.

"I had a most disturbing dream, Glen, that my presence was greatly needed at home. In it, I saw something dark and sinister had come upon our lands, and I came in all haste. I am sorry that I was not able to collect everything on your list, but I do believe I have most of what you requested. I found an abundance of Sassafras and decided to bring it along. I took special care to pack it away as you instructed me about the other plants. Do you know of this darkness? Tell me that what I speak of is not true, Glen."

"I am distraught with sorrow, Luther." She took a cleansing breath then told Lutherian of all the trouble in the garden, her dream of her father, and the list of feys and fairies needed to remove her mother from her crystal prison.

"I am not sure of the origins of this darkness, only of the destruction it has caused, Luther."

"This is all so unbelievable, and I am still trying to wrap my head around all you have said, Glen. You say Kim is with Queen Joyce?"

"Yes, Luther, and I need her to come with me, Green, White, and Pink to the Garden of Rarities to find that plant straightaway. Please help me send her this request. Sit with me."

Lutherian sat with Glenlillian, and they joined their minds to seek out their daughter. The words "Come home quickly" floated in the wind and blew toward Fitzhuwlyn Castle, entered a window, and glided in search of Kim Gold Fairy to come in all haste.

After the initial shock of seeing a fairy for the first time, for she could not remember meeting Kim and her daughters, Agnes did not answer Kim's question straightaway. Shaking her head to clear her mind, she finally spoke.

"I am sorry, Kim. Could you repeat your question?"

"I am wondering if you remember anything at all about your past. Even the smallest inkling could help you regain your memory," Kim said as she raised her eyebrows.

"I am sorry, Kim. I have resigned myself to the fact that I will not regain my memory, and this revelation has calmed me. I can now look forward to creating new memories and deciding on my future. I have been received here in this wondrous place with open arms, but I cannot overstay my welcome. I must find a place to live and work. I do not wish to become a burden to these lovely people, no matter how much they insist I stay. Do you think you can convince the queen that I need to make my own way?" Agnes asked.

"I believe I can do what you ask."

Taking a moment, Kim paused. Then she widened her eyes as she thought of solving two problems at one time and smiled.

"I happen to know of a place you can live and work. It is deep in a wooded area with a recently built cottage. It has a grand meadow and a little river that flows into an open hidden lake. There is a…"

Kim paused a moment to ponder how to explain Mirrorme to Agnes, and then continued. "There is a female creature that lives alone in that area who would welcome the company of another. She is very knowledgeable in the gathering of special plants and herbs that cure some of the ills and complaints of humans. Her name is Mirrorme, and she is a land mermaid. I call her Meme for short, and she is a wonderfully kind and thoughtful creature. She expressed to me that she needed a human to take the gathered plants to a trading post at North/Southland. It is a popular place for buying and trading, and I understand they are particularly low on the chamomile plant used for a calming tea. Do you think that would be something you would be interested in?"

"Oh, yes, Kim. It is a glorious idea. I cannot wait to meet Meme and begin a new life for myself. How can I thank you properly for this unbelievable kindness?"

Kim pushed the sound of her mother and father's urgent words to come home away from her mind, and then finished her conversation with Agnes.

"You can thank me by not speaking to the queen about all we have discussed. Also, you need to be patient and wait until I have also had the opportunity to speak with Meme about this idea. Many things can go wrong or minds may change before this can happen. Can you do that, Agnes? Can you hold your own counsel?"

"Yes, Kim. I promise to hold my tongue, my thoughts, and to be patient until you return with confirmation that Meme agrees," Agnes said.

Agnes could not help herself and gently hugged the fairy. Kim smiled and spoke in a rush.

"I must leave you now, for I have urgent business to attend elsewhere."

Kim nodded and left Agnes to ponder all that was said to her.

The knock at her sleeping room door broke her thoughts, and she answered, "Come in." Maggie balanced the tray of food in one hand and opened the door with the other. Agnes quickly approached the elderly servant and removed the tray of food from her hands. As she placed the tray on the bedside table, she spoke with sincere words.

"Oh, Maggie, there is no need for you to serve me as if I were royalty. I believe it is time I helped out around here. I cannot with good conscience lounge about. Please let me help you with your tasks. I am strong and would love to help with the cleaning. This is a large place to keep up with, and I, for one, would love the distraction. My memory is gone, and there is no need for me to think on the unpleasant nature of it all. Come sit with me and share what you have brought."

Poor Maggie could only nod her yes, for she was truly speechless and could not think of a proper reply to the kind suggestion from the woman who no longer resembled the old Agnes. Maggie had not noticed until then how different in appearance Agnes looked. Her hair was a lovely, long, glossy brown. Her eyes were no longer black in appearance but a light shade of blue, and her smile was genuine. As Maggie and Agnes shared the meal, they spoke of things needing to be done and right there they became good friends.

# Chapter Ten

im appeared before her parents in the quickest of moments. Before she could utter one word, she flew to her father and hugged him so hard he began to cough.

"Kim, unloose your father before he passes out from your enthusiasm," Glenlillian uttered.

Green, Pink, and White Fairy giggled, and then stopped after Kim gave them a stern look. Setting Kim at arm's length, he spoke with a smile upon his face.

"Huw is putting your mother's things in the storage shed and will be along shortly. Your other daughters are scattered about doing the things requested of them. But you, Glen, Pink, White, and Green must go on a search this very moment for the double-healing plant. Glen knows where it is, and you must collect the leaves in all haste and bring them here."

Huw floated to Glenlillian and handed her the large pot filled with Sassafras.

"I have added the other ingredients as you requested, Glenlillian."

"Thank you, Huw." Huw nodded, smiled, and then floated to Kim.

After he kissed Kim, Glenlillian, and his grandfairies, Lutherian commanded, "Go, now!"

As they quietly approached the Garden of Rarities, White Fairy spoke with sadness and fear. "Mother, Grandmother, the first group of Crystal Butterflies are nearing Phenloris. There is no food for them to eat, and they do not have the strength to fly to Coremerick to feed. We need to stall them somehow."

"Where are they exactly, White?" Glenlillian questioned.

"They come by way of Bardfey Island."

"Give me your hands quickly." Joining hands, they listened to Glenlillian speak her words of chanting.

"Come most wondrous wizard of old, come here to the place of the garden foretold; in ancient times alive with life, we call out to you for help this night. Come, Merddlyn, come!"

With a clash of lightning and roaring thunder the wizard stood before the hovering fairies and bellowed his words, "Glenlillian Crystal Fairy, what in all the heavens have you done?"

Then he did a most unexpected thing. He roared with laughter until tears rolled down his face.

Kim, White, Green, and Pink Fairy could only stare in wonder at the wizard.

"That was quite well done, Glenlillian. Please tell me why I have been so unceremoniously brought here?"

Glenlillian grabbed the wizard and held him tightly to her. The tears she had held in for so long could no longer be contained and spilled freely down her face. Merddlyn cooed softly spoken words of comfort and continued to hold her until she was ready to speak.

"You say they approach Bardfey, White?"

"Yes, Merddlyn. As we speak they come near the center of the island."

"Good. Now, I need you all to hover around me quickly."

They did as Merddlyn requested.

"I will put the butterflies to sleep, suspended in time. They will lay gently upon the tall weeds and minimal grasses hidden and safe. I need all of you to see this in your minds, to use your unique gifts to join with mine to make this so."

In one fairy moment, it was done.

A great calmness came over the fairies, but Merddlyn spoke words of caution.

"Glenlillian, we must find Meirionwen in all haste after you locate the double-healing plant. We all know that she is the one who can undo the calamity here, and I will do all I can to stop the portents of doom from falling upon this land. Meirionwen is the one who should handle the butterflies once they come out of their suspension. Since she is the one who awakened them those many years ago, they will remember her, and I am sure they will be happy to see her once again. The Crystal Butterflies are comfortable for the moment, but they can break free of the suspension once they realize they have been delayed. We have three, maybe four risings of the moon before they are able to break our spell." Glenlillian nodded and spoke of her dream.

"Then we must gather all in haste and go to the place of her encasement. It is not a coincidence that the butterflies are so close to the cave where Meirionwen resides," the wizard said.

"Merddlyn, once I have removed the leaves from the double-healing plant, we will need to return home to gather all the other healing herbs and put them in as many containers as we can carry. Kim can take us quickly to our storage room, and I will speak with Huw and Luther about gathering up the other fairies."

Turning to Kim, Glenlillian spoke with concern etched in her voice. "I have not seen Brown anywhere. Do you know where she is?"

"Yes. She is in the deep forest speaking with Meme. I cannot go to her and to our storage room at the same time."

"I will collect Brown," Merddlyn announced.

"No. That is not necessary. Besides, I do not think she would be comfortable seeing your approach. I am quite certain she would fly from you. I can tell Meme what I need, and she can inform Brown to head to Bardfey Island in all haste and meet us there," Kim finished.

Glenlillian nodded her approval and all the fairies glided in a line to seek out the hiding plant as Merddlyn walked behind them.

In a quiet voice, Green Fairy said, "There you are sweet plant."

Glenlillian and the others approached in quiet adoration. Speaking in a calm apologetic voice, Glenlillian knelt down and slowly poured the Sassafras syrup over the plant.

"Forgive me most wondrous plant. I was not responsible for all the destruction you see around you. I am in great need of your help and require five leaves from you to heal a special fairy that is at this very moment encased in crystal. Your leaves are to be mixed with other healing herbs and pastes that will heal her severe wound as she is gently removed and awakened."

As Glenlillian poured more of the Sassafras syrup on the soil around the plant, it began to grow. Taller now then the shriveled weeds around it, the plant put out her inner leaves and coaxed Glenlillian to remove them. With a gentle hand, she broke the leaves off and placed them in a small sack that was tied to her dress. Immediately, five new leaves replaced the missing ones, and the plant bowed down to Glenlillian Crystal Fairy. Green Fairy poured the last of the Sassafras around the plant and gently patted the soil, packing it tightly around the plant. Then she bent down and placed a soft kiss on a leaf. Immediately it grabbed Green Fairy in a strong hug, patted her head with its longest leaf, and whispered words only Green Fairy could hear.

"Thank you." Satisfied that the plant was renewed, she hovered next to her sisters, mother, and grandmother.

"I must go back to my meeting, Glen," Merddlyn said. "And I would appreciate it if you would send me back the way I came."

Glenlillian nodded and motioned the fairies to circle her once again. Speaking the words of movement, she sent Merddlyn back to his meeting place.

"Are you ready?" Queen Joyce questioned Teri.

"Yes." Teri smiled.

"You look lovely, princess." Siomara wiped at a tear. "Your gown sparkles all over like splendid jewels, and your small diamond tiara and veil are simply stunning. I still cannot believe you have asked me to be your best maid. I do believe Sara was in shock when I told her you wanted her in your wedding as well. It is such an honor for both of us, Teri."

Sara, Fitzhuwlyn's resident flower girl, could not speak and smiled shyly at Siomara's words.

Turning to Agnes, Siomara continued, "And you look lovely, Agnes. That dress matches your blue eyes, and your hair looks splendid pulled up in that cornet."

Agnes smiled and with breathless speech said, "I am truly grateful that you have included me in this most wonderful celebration. My new memories are of such goodness, wonder, and kindness that I am overwhelmed with gratitude. Thank you, Queen Joyce, for not throwing me out when you came upon me in your kitchen. Thank you, princess, for not handing me over to the servants who clearly wanted to dump me in the soup. Also, thank you, Siomara, for loaning me this beautiful dress. I believe we three match quite nicely."

All the women hugged; and with a nod from the queen, all five women walked into the newly built chapel within sight of the garden and meadow near Fitzhuwlyn Castle.

Among the assembled were King Crawford, Myles, Christopher, Jahaziel, Gauwain, the servants of Fitzhuwlyn Castle, and Myles's parents, Mr. and Mrs. Albright.

Queen Joyce quickly sat next to King Crawford and received a gentle squeeze on her hand and his smile.

Myles walked to the chapel entrance to meet his bride. Taking her hand, he raised it to his lips and slowly kissed each finger then whispered, "The sight of you takes my breath away and I am speechless."

Princess Teri glanced at her lovely dried flower arrangement and fought back the tears that began to form. Taking in a slow breath, she smiled brightly at her husband-to-be.

Walking hand in hand they passed the assembled. A unified gasp was heard from the women present and smiles could not be contained by the men.

Princess Teri's dress sparkled with the help of the noon day sun peeking through the evenly spaced, small, square openings that lined the walls of the chapel. Her veil, held in place by the silver and jeweled tiara, cascaded to the floor as it met the train of her wedding gown. When they reached the prayer altar, Myles and Teri turned around to face their family and friends.

Everyone stood at the sound of the flute and harp being played by two young servants. Sara was pleased with the dried flower arrangements she created for all four of them. Keeping time to the music, she slowly walked in holding her arrangement so tightly that her hands shook. With a shy smile, she was ceremoniously met by Christopher, who escorted her down the aisle. Next was Agnes, who was holding a duplicate arrangement and was joined by Sir Jahaziel. Last was Siomara who was holding a slightly different arrangement. She could not help the smile when she looked at Sir Gauwain. With a fair blush upon her face, she caught his wink.

As the couples approached the prayer altar of the chapel, they separated. The women stood to the left, and the men stood to the right.

When the music stopped, Retreat Servant Bartholomew coughed, and then spoke rather quietly.

"We are all assembled here to witness the marriage of Myles and Princess Teri. However, before I continue, King Crawford has a few words to say."

King Crawford stood, walked to the front near the small altar, turned around, and began his speech.

"Myles, would you stand before me please?"

Myles's eyes opened wide, but he did as his king commanded. "If you do not mind, son, please kneel." Myles knelt, but his eyes did not move from Teri's deceptively calm countenance.

King Crawford removed his ceremonial jeweled saber and gently touched Myles's left then right shoulder and spoke with gentle words.

"I, King Crawford William Martin George Fitzhuwlyn, king of the Realm, North, South, East, West, of the great forest, land holder of King Edward's Allenwood Castle and domain, and protector of the land of Newry, do hereby bestow upon Myles Anthony Albright the title of prince and knight of Allenwood." Once again, the king gently tapped Myles's left and right shoulders, and then finished his words. "Please stand, Prince Myles." The moment he stood, the crowd roared with delight, and the king hugged his soon-to-be son-in-law.

Myles turned to Teri and said in a whisper, "You knew about this and did not tell me?" Her giggle gave him his answer. As the king went back to his bench seat, Myles stood once again next to his princess.

As the ceremony ended, everyone gave their well wishes to the newlyweds. The entire wedding party and assembled guests went into the castle to eat, drink, and enjoy what was left of the day. No one noticed the absence of flowers or plants. No one complained about the rather bland fare from the lack of herbs or the tasteless shriveled fruit decorating the wedding table. It was all a splendid affair as far as Teri was concerned. She leaned once again into Myles's side and spoke words of love. All the guests were comfortably seated at the many tables beautifully arranged and covered with a variety of colored cloths. The wedding party could be viewed by all enjoying their fare as they sat to the left, right, and center of Teri and Myles at the long table. Teri's smile faded slightly as a conspiratorial thought came to her, and she whispered her words to Myles with enthusiasm.

"Myles, do you not think Gauwain and Siomara, Christopher and Sara, and Jahaziel and Agnes make great couples?" His only answer was to spit out every ounce of mead he had just begun to drink, nearly choking in the process.

Agnes left her place at the table and gracefully walked toward Maggie, who was refilling several wine goblets. Jahaziel's eyes followed her, and he did not realize he was smiling. Just moments ago she had spoken her concerns to him about the busy servants not being able to join in the festivities and decided to help them out with the serving and cleaning up. She told Jahaziel that they had just as much of a right to sit, eat, and enjoy the day as everyone else did. Her smile was breathtaking when she approached Maggie, and her hug genuine.

Jahaziel began to brood when he realized his thoughts were heading in a direction he did not want them to go.

"I should have stayed at Allenwood," he mumbled.

The knight was well into his second cup of mead when Christopher approached the table. He spoke a bit harshly, and Christopher's eyebrows rose in question at Jahaziel's statement.

"I know who she looks like, Christopher. I am hoping it is not the same woman who walked with me down that isle. It cannot be the same woman. How is this possible? It is as if she has been recreated and changed back to her former self and much improved. Although I did not see the other Agnes before Kim sent her to that prison, I was given an accounting of how drastically she had changed and that no trace of who she was before remained. Now she is back to the way I remember her from years ago.

"She was a beautiful, tall, unique, opinionated, young woman not much older than Siomara. Agnes nearly clobbered me senseless with a wine goblet many years ago when I said something she and Siomara found inappropriate. Lucky for me, I ducked just in time." Jahaziel chuckled at the memory. "What say you, Christopher? Is this the same woman?"

Jahaziel's eyes rose to meet Christopher's. He did not expect the bright smile or the cocky attitude.

"Are you starting to have feelings for Agnes, Jahaziel?" Christopher quipped.

Jahaziel stood too quickly. The chair flew backward and hit the wall behind him. With a loud crack, it broke into pieces. Jahaziel's roar was deafening and Christopher's yell began to fade as he ran out of the hall with Jahaziel quickly closing in behind him.

# Chapter Eleven

irrorme was deep in conversation with Brown Fairy when suddenly she stopped her thoughts and held up one hand. She shook her head at Brown Fairy.

*Kim speaks to me, Brown. She says you must go to Bardfey Island now. Some of your sisters, Glenlillian, Luther, Huw, and another will join you as soon as they are able. You are to approach from the north end of the island and only the north. You are to stay within sight of the moors of the original site of Phenloris. Kim asks if you understand.*

"I understand your words, Meme, but I do not understand the reason. Ask her please."

*She says there is no time to explain, but you must hurry. Would you like me to run along with you?*

"Yes, that would keep me from thinking dark thoughts. Thank you, Meme."

*Kim says I may accompany you, but I must turn back at the meeting meadow. You are to remain hidden until Kim approaches.*

Brown Fairy quickly floated next to Mirrorme, who ran along a path that headed in the direction of the island.

Mirrorme raised her hand to Brown Fairy to stop. She was breathing hard and needed to catch her breath. She leaned over at the waist and braced a large oak with her right hand; her left hand was on her left knee. Finally, with her breathing slowing, she was able to mind speak.

*Brown, how much further do you think the island is? I cannot run much farther. I need to rest just a moment or two more.*

"I am sorry, but there is a bit more distance I must go to reach it, Meme. You can stay here, and I will be fine to go on my own."

Mirrorme shook her head quickly back and forth, sending her thoughts once again.

*No. I promised Kim I would go with you and watch until you reach the northern end of the moors. I will keep my promise, Brown.*

In a show of comfort and friendship, Brown Fairy patted Mirrorme's back to calm her and said, "Okay, I can wait a bit longer. Are you hungry? Would you like me to fetch you something to eat?"

Mirrorme began to laugh in her mind and sent her thoughts to Brown Fairy.

*What is it with all you fairies obsessing over feeding me? Look at me. That is why I cannot run as fast or as far as before.*

Brown Fairy and Mirrorme laughed out loud, but only Brown Fairy's laughter could be heard floating upon the wind.

Mawrthlyn stumbled in the darkness. His exhaustion was apparent, and his slow movements did not alleviate the pain he felt. He grabbed Maximillian by his shirt collar and spoke with harsh words.

"Find us something to eat, you brain-empty oaf."

As Maximillian flew to do his bidding, Mawrthlyn brooded about the fight with the elf. The battle had lasted too long in his estimation. He recalled the incident.

*Darrius had ventured out close to Castle Mead looking for the rubber trees that did not grow in the Newry Valley. It was often used to waterproof boats, doors, roofs, and rope ladders when the harsh winds blew, and the snow fell upon their lands. Pleased with the amount of sap collected, he bent down to lift the wooden keg filled with liquid rubber with the intent of loading it onto a cart harnessed to his old horse.*

*A sound caught his attention, and he quickly stood. Frozen in motion, he blinked his eyes and beheld a very tall black-robed individual within arm's length. As it quickly drew a sword to fight, Darrius did the same.*

*The clashing sound of metal upon metal echoed into the forest, and Darrius's cart-harnessed horse ran in the direction of home and safety. The grunts and groans from Darrius lessened as his weakened state from blood loss became evident.*

*Mawrthlyn was in no better shape, as Darrius had sliced him in several places, but he gathered the last of his strength and brought forth a bolt of lightning. Mawrthlyn threw it forward, and it hit Darrius in the center of his chest. Flying backward at great speed, the elf did not stop until he hit a large oak. His lifeless body slammed hard against the wood, and he slid down to its base. His slumped body smoked in various places from the charring.*

*With his strength completely depleted, Mawrthlyn fell to the ground covered in his own blood and the hooded robe. Closing his eyes, he slipped into unconsciousness and did not wake for several long moments.*

The fey flitted into the encampment he had prepared for his captor's comfort. He whimpered in pain each time he set his feet on the ground to bend down. He was reluctant to build a fire to roast the rabbits he recently snared, but he ignored his pain lest he be beaten again. His minimal thoughts could not understand his captor's constant anger. He would lash Maximillian many times for not doing his bidding quickly enough, and the fey guard dared not ask the figure what his name was, for then he would be called every insulting thing except his own name. There was no comfort to be found in the company of the dark figure called Master, and he feared for his life. Not once did Maximillian try to escape. He knew Master would find him. He knew the worst possible punishment would be his own death.

He could not help the tears streaming down his face as he looked transfixed at the low burning fire and the roasting rabbits. He did not like the smell of the cooked rabbits and wondered if he had ever eaten such things. As his mind wandered once again, he tried to stop his thoughts from going back to their first meeting but he could not. Resigned, he went into his first memories.

*Abject fear was the first feeling he became aware of when he awakened. The extremely tall, dark figure was standing before him yelling at him to rise up over and over again. The words were slowly understood, and he did as he was commanded to do and flitted up with shaking wings.*

*"You mindless twit. Could you not hear my bellowing? I am Master, and you are my servant. You will do all that I say, or I will kill you. Do you understand my words?"*

*He nodded but dared not speak. He flitted behind the darkly clothed figure but dared not mention that they were going in circles through a densely wooded area. Master seemed confused, and when he sat down to gather his thoughts and center his mind to their whereabouts, he commanded Maximillian to sit next to him. He smiled, hoping for a little comfort and explanation. Then Master struck him in the face.*

The snapping of twigs brought him back to the present, and Maximillian busied himself with preparing the rest of the meal.

Richmond, Farian, Egwin, and Linden were arguing with one another when a flash of light caught their attention, and their complaining stopped at the sight of Merddlyn standing before them once again.

"It is a shame, Merddlyn, that I cannot see with my own eyes the look of shock upon the faces of Egwin, Linden, and Farian. I can imagine it to be quite memorable."

Richmond laughed a hardy laugh as the now familiar sound of shouting tumbled around them.

Merddlyn raised his eyes to the ceiling of Richmond's sitting room, hoping they would all come to their senses and just be quiet.

Giving up that he would ever be able to speak with calm words among all the shouting, Merddlyn walked to Richmond's food preparation room and set a pot on the iron grate in his fireplace. It always had a low burning fire available for Richmond to cook on and to enjoy its welcoming warmth. The handy water jug had been recently filled, and he poured the water into the pot and waited for it to boil. *Tea,* he thought, *will be a welcome distraction from these emotional elves.* His patience was wearing thin, and he commanded the water to boil. Closing his eyes, Merddlyn enjoyed the first sips of tea and waited for the elves to join him.

⌇

"Oh, Myles, everything is so beautiful." Princess Teri did not realize tears of joy were streaming down her face as she looked upon the many changes to the interior of Allenwood Castle. "Christopher must have worked himself to exhaustion fixing all the problems and deterioration."

"Yes, I believe he and his workmen did, sweetheart. Come with me. You have to see the sleeping room. It has a ceiling again, and we do not have to peer at the stars from our bed and pray it does not rain."

Teri laughed until her sides hurt, and Myles pulled her along. Their laughter could be heard echoing down the many halls of the castle as they went to every room, every hallway, and finally ended up in the kitchen. They sat at the table with the matching wooden stools where there was a single piece of parchment paper with writing, and upon that lavish handwritten note rested a beautiful red rose. Myles picked up the rose and handed it to Teri. Then he read the note aloud.

*Prince Myles, Princess Teri. Please accept my gift of congratulations on your marriage. I made the table and chairs for my own kitchen months ago but realized they were too small for the area and built another much larger set. I give it to you freely and hope you enjoy its comfort for years to come. A cozy warm kitchen is a wonderful place for private conversation.*

It was signed, Sir Gauwain.

"Myles, this was so thoughtful of Sir Gauwain, but where do you suppose he found this beautiful rose?" Teri took a sniff. "It smells wonderful."

He took the rose from Teri's hand and inhaled deeply. "Yes. It smells positively delicious. I have missed this smell and the smells of other flowers." Seeing the tears in Teri's eyes, he quickly added, "Do not cry, Teri. I am sure everyone is doing what they can to right this wrong that was so cruelly thrust upon us. I have complete trust in all the fairies that they can turn the tide of change in our favor. Come. You are tired and need sleep."

In silence, they walked hand in hand to their sleeping room, and Myles quietly shut the door behind them.

White Fairy began to get flashes of something she did not understand. As she moved through the wrinkle of time, she heard the sound of words floating all around her, softly at first. It seemed to be a whisper; and then the words came closer, louder, and stronger in their intensity. White Fairy clearly understood what was being said to her, and she continued to move through time, not by her own desire to do so, but by an unknown force pulling her. The words repeated themselves over and over again until she reached the place where the force intended her to be.

*He is in danger. He will be killed. You must help him. Again, he is in danger. He will be killed. You must help him. Again...*

Kim went into a panic when White Fairy faded before everyone's eyes. Just as suddenly, Orange Fairy approached with cautious flitting.

Before anyone could speak, Orange Fairy said in a whisper, "I have been given an understanding, not in words but in thought, that I was needed here. I have been following all of you, and I am happy to have caught up with everyone."

When White Fairy reappeared, she was shaking, crying hysterically, and fell to the ground. She was immediately surrounded by Glenlillian, Kim, Green, Orange, and Pink Fairy, and they hugged her until the sobbing stopped.

When her hiccups began, she spoke with a strained voice. "Where is Brown? We need her help, Mother."

Looking at Kim, White Fairy began to cry again. Glenlillian held her in a strong hug and whispered the soothing words of the birthing song, and then answered her question.

"Brown is on her way, sweetling, and should arrive shortly." Finally calm enough to speak, White Fairy told them what she had come upon.

"I do not know how I was pulled through time against my own will, but I heard words of warning that someone was about to die. I shook off my fear and gave in to it. When I reached the intended place, I saw Maximillian sitting by a fire. He was crying, and he looked as if he had been badly beaten. Blood was all over his clothing, and he was shaking but not from the cold night air, rather from fear. I do not know who beat him, but we have very little time to aid in his escape. We must help him!"

White Fairy could not stop the new flow of tears, but she was no longer in the hysterical state she had been in just moments before. As Brown Fairy flitted through a thicket, White Fairy jumped up and flew to her sister. Striking her hard, they fell to the ground with a loud thump, and Brown

Fair had just enough time to roll them away from the spiked Newberry Bush.

Brown Fairy rose up, still holding on to White Fairy and hovered before everyone with questioning eyes. Kim repeated everything White Fairy had said so that Brown Fairy could better understand her sister's panic.

When she spoke, it was more like a command. "I can lift Max. White can take us back to the encampment. Orange, you need to make us invisible, and Pink, you need to turn on your wing lights so we can see in this darkness. Grandmother, you and Mother must put him to sleep, because Red is not here to help us at the moment."

"Yes I am." Red Fairy burst through the thicket and hovered before everyone, and then held up her hand for silence. "Do you all seriously think that I would not know something terrible is happening? I am as much a part of this as all of you and know my presence here is imperative. The voice spoke to me to come in all haste. Who called to me?" Red Fairy questioned.

"I asked Luther and Huw to fetch the rest of you. Was it him you heard calling?" Glenlillian questioned. Red Fairy shook her head no.

"I do not know or understand this voice you and White speak of, Red, but we do not have time for a discussion. Now, let us save Maximillian in all haste. Kim and I will wait here and prepare the healing herbs for him. Red, you make sure he does not awaken too quickly." Glenlillian ended her words and nodded for the fairies to go.

The fey was in so much pain, he could not eat the unappetizing brown fruit he came upon earlier. He knew Master would return shortly, and his fear grew with every passing moment. The approaching dark clouds blocked out the crescent moon, adding to his fear, so he closed his eyes. A sound was closing in behind him, and panic rose in his throat. He prayed it was not Master returning to beat him once again.

When he felt a soft touch on his forehead, Maximillian opened his eyes and beheld a beautiful creature. Then sleep claimed him.

"You come back here as quickly as you can after you deliver Max to Luther, White. Brown, are you sure you can hold on to him?"

Brown Fairy did not answer Glenlillian's question, but she did give her a strange look. She had grown taller and stronger than any fairy in the history of the clans, and because of this, she was called upon to assist with various tasks when feys were away exploring other lands. Brown Fairy adjusted Maximillian over her shoulder once more and nodded to White Fairy that she was ready. In the twinkling of a bright star, they were gone.

Moments later, Yellow, Blue, and Purple Fairy were hovering together asking the same question Red Fairy had asked moments ago. "Who called us to come here in all haste, Mother?"

Jahaziel's head pounded, and he stumbled to the table to fill a cup with water. He had moved his personal belongings out of Allenwood Castle the night before the wedding and claimed a nearby empty hut for himself. Christopher had assisted him with the few pieces of furniture he owned, and he was satisfied with the results as he looked around. His bed was centered at the north-facing wall hidden behind a large partition that was hand painted by his sister. It depicted skillfully done scenes of a beautiful meadow surrounded by woods that were filled with hiding animals. Jahaziel had not known his sister could paint, and he remembered her laughing at him when he failed to find all the hidden creatures.

The large quilt was a gift from Queen Joyce, and he walked over to it, picked it up off the floor, and haphazardly placed in back on the bed. Two book stands stood at each side of the huge bed, and a sea chest was at the foot. A long, light-blue curtain covered the only window in the hut situated on the west wall next to the front entrance. The hearth no longer held the warmth of a fire—it had gone out in the early morning hours. Walking back to the table, he poured his water, took a long drink and then sat down on the stool. *How much did I drink at the wedding?* he wondered. It was not like him to indulge in wine, mead, and beer. Then he groaned recalling the reason. Agnes.

Standing quickly, Jahaziel decided an early morning swim in the nearby lake was in order. After that, he would seek out his sister for a quick meal.

The swim cleared his head, and he quickly dressed in the dry clothes he had brought with him. The task gave him time to ponder on Agnes. He could not for the life of him understand the strange pounding of his heart and his loss for words whenever she was in sight. As he approached Fitzhuwlyn Castle's entrance, he began to bellow Siomara's name.

"Stop your shouting, Jahaziel. We can hear you all the way out to the bailey. The sun is just this moment on the rise, and you will wake everyone inside still sleeping." The "we" became apparent as Agnes walked alongside his sister. There was a lovely smile on her lips and a gentle sway to her hips as she approached. With the soft pink of a blush on her face, she curtisied. When she looked directly at Jahaziel with those beautiful light-blue eyes, he knew he was a doomed man.

Lutherian was in deep conversation with Huw, Broadwayne, and Cassiarian when Brown Fairy entered the weapons hut with the sleeping Maximillian over a shoulder. She gently set the fey down on a bed near a corner, and then turned to face Lutherian.

She quickly placed a finger to her lips for everyone to be quiet, and then said softly, "He is asleep for now but will awaken soon enough. I must tell you quickly that Max does not know who he is, where he comes from, nor does he remember anything from his past. We are waiting for you to come with White and me to Bardfey Island, Grandfather. There is no need for you to seek out the rest of my sisters because they are already there."

Before Brown Fairy could finish, Lutherian spoke in hushed words. "I understand what you are saying Brown, but start at the beginning of this tale so Broadwayne and Cassiarian may better understand our predicament."

She told them everything she knew about the problems with the gardens and how White Fairy found Maximillian. She finished her words with the imperative plea for Lutherian to come with her and White Fairy back to Bardfey Island that moment. Turning to Huw, she addressed him. "Huw, you must grab the mesquite harp and come with us as well." Everyone turned when Kim glided in, hugged Huw, and spoke to Broadwayne and Cassiarian while she was still lovingly held in Huw's arms.

"Both of you must take care of Max. We have bound up his wounds, but the bandages will need to be changed. Be careful what you say in his presence; and for all the heaven's sake, do not speak of his past misdeeds. Do you understand me? Have a care Cassiarian and Broadwayne; he is in a fragile state."

They nodded together and left quickly to gather food, honey-dipped cloths, and wine for Maximillian.

Lutherian approached Kim and lovingly touched the side of her face while he spoke. "You cannot take us all back to the island, Kim. You may not heal well with the weight of us once we reach our destination. Not to mention, Huw's harp weighs more than all of us put together. We need to think of another way to get there quickly."

Kim smiled and said, "Come with me, Father."

Her smile had Lutherian on guard, but when they floated out of the weapons hut, Lutherian sucked in his breath. Elaine and Enos were swishing their tales back and forth to the sound of music heard only by the unicorns. Each nodded to Lutherian in greeting.

Kim spoke while patting the pair. "You and Huw can fly quickly on the unicorns to the island. There are patches of sweet grass near the entrance of the cave where they can feed, and I have asked them to stand guard to alert us if anything is amiss."

Kim handed Huw a rope she had confiscated from Jahaziel long ago. She liked how it felt, and its strength was more than adequate for the purpose of securing the harp to one of the unicorn's backs.

## Part Four
### The Destroyers of Darkness

# Chapter Twelve

Long ago, in a land no longer remembered, there was a secret elfin society known as the Destroyers of Darkness. They hunted an ancient evil no longer dormant or bound.

Free from its prison and filled with rage, it roamed unnoticed through the many fairylands by the cover of night. Determined and without conscience, the darkness focused in on its greatest desire: eliminate every human from the land until no human remains.

Now it was the destiny of this society to capture, and once again, imprison this evil before it reached its goal in this darkest of quests.

"Where are we, Egwin?" Linden complained.

"I believe we are approaching the base of the Newry Mountains by way of the hidden valley."

"What!" Linden hollered. "If I knew we were going home to collect supplies, I would have gathered the necessary goods I have been collecting these last days to drop off at my cousin Alwyn's home. He and Willa are running low on some spices I promised months ago." Linden ended his words in a huff.

"When have you had time to collect spices? Are you deliberately trying to vex me, Linden? That is a female chore." Egwin ended his words with laughter.

"Are you finished laughing at me, Egwin? Your insults are not appreciated. How dare you call me a woman. I believe you have been in the company of fairies far too long. And where do you suppose Farian and Merddlyn are by now?"

As the sun rose high in the sky, the small boat gently came ashore with the waves pushing it onto the sand and crushed seashell-laden beach.

"Speaking of your cousin, how is Alwyn?" Egwin asked.

"He and Willa are doing well. The mourning period is over and they have moved into his father's home. Darrius will be missed by many."

"Yes, Linden, he will truly be missed." Both elves remained quiet, thinking of the day Darrius's body was found half-hidden under dense brush.

It had been a deliberate murder and from the look of him, he had fought well and hard to save his own life. In ceremonious sorrow, his body and sword were given to Alwyn to prepare him for burial. As the sun began to rise, Darrius was gently placed into the ground. Surrounded by generations of family long gone, Darrius could finally rest from a hard, well-lived life. A long life filled with many battles lost and won, laughter and music, love, family, community, and prayer. With quiet song, his name had been added to the list of family names that had gone before him. As the sun burst forth, a roar of cheer had gone up with raised swords and voices, as elves from near and far honored him with their last farewell.

Darrius was a huge elf, tall and muscular. He was a great warrior, who had been given the honor by the council of elves to train the strongest for battle. His face and body had many scars to show that he had taken his appointment to heart.

Alwyn vowed to find whoever was responsible for the death of his father. If it took him to the ends of the valley and beyond, he would not stop until he was found and brought back to face the judgment of the court. However, there were no clues to follow, foot prints to track, or blood trailing the direction the killer had gone. Darrius's body was covered with long gashes and blackened skin marked him in various places, as if he had been burned. Alwyn's insight had been blocked, and he could not understand why. Finally, a council meeting was convened to discuss Darrius's death. Many male and female elves were in attendance; and after a long discussion, they joined their insight to focus their minds to seek the perpetrator and his or her whereabouts. To their great sorrow, they saw only darkness.

Feeling better then he had in days, King William packed up a sack filled with food and wine and two goblets as well as the gift he had carved himself. Mounting his horse, he reminded himself to go slow. His cousin Queen Joyce would box his ears if she knew his plans for the trip had begun so soon after his illness finally left him. He had been told by Joyce to rest as much as he was able to tolerate, and she made a promise to return to check on him. He laughed out loud thinking on how her face would look if she made good her word and found him missing. His destination was just past the magical land of Newry where he had come upon the unicorns those many months ago.

Alwyn walked to the edge of the forest near the Eastern Ocean and waited for the king. His insight told him William was on his way.

He did not want his wife, Willa, to follow, so he made the excuse to fetch clams for their dinner to ensure she would not. She disliked clam hunting with a passion. His friendship with the king began with his search for the missing baby unicorns. A myth had come true in the whispers of forest creatures. The guinea cava, Patrice, told him the story of the sad birth and of a human who walked their land.

The twin unicorns were born next to their dead father, and their mother refused to leave him or look for nourishment for the three of them. The twins were able to feed for three days before their mother died. With strength enough to stand and wander, they sought help from the forests birds, squirrels, rabbits, and guinea cavas. At last, a tall, strange-looking creature stood still at the edge of the land, a short distance beyond the land of Newry. This land was the land of elves, and they went to the creature unafraid and hungry.

"Ah, there you are, William," Alwyn spoke.

"Yes, here I am, and I wonder why you have asked for this meeting. The messenger you sent told me nothing," William replied.

"I need your help, William." Alwyn spoke in a tired voice, and then continued. "Normally, I would not involve humans in my own affairs, and if I am found seeking help from you, I could ultimately be banished from home and land."

William's eyes widened, but he said nothing in response to that surprising statement.

"I understand you are quite good at solving puzzles and are a seeker of truth. Is this so, William?"

"I am told by others that I am successful in these matters. What is it you wish me to find Alwyn?"

Alwyn's eyes became dark and his face had no smile when he spoke. "I need you to help me find my father's murderer."

King William looked at his friend with serious eyes and nodded.

"Start at the beginning, Alwyn, and leave nothing out," the king replied.

Quiet moments passed as the king thought on the matter of Darrius.

"I need you to take me to the place of his downfall, Alwyn. I know this will be difficult, but I need to look around the area." William held up his hand to stop Alwyn from speaking, and then continued. "I know everyone has done their best to find clues, but I have a fresh perspective and fresh eyes with which to look around. Who knows what I may come upon?" With a jolt, William and Alwyn turned around with swords in hand at the sound of approaching footsteps.

As Egwin and Linden approached the elf and human speaking to one another, they drew their sword and mace for battle.

"Egwin!" Alwyn roared. "What the blazes are you doing here?"

Nearly simultaneously, Egwin roared, "What is that human doing here?"

"Let us all lower our weapons. There is no trouble here," King William said with cautious words.

"Be careful of your words here, Alwyn. This human's presence alone, along with any words spoken here, cannot be taken back and would ultimately bring dishonor upon us all."

"You think me an idiot, Egwin!" Alwyn roared.

Linden stepped between his cousin and Egwin and nearly shouted himself. "Stop this shouting at once, Egwin. Let Alwyn speak." Egwin nodded and apologized but spoke with tense lips. "Who is this human, Alwyn?"

"I can speak for myself, Alwyn." He stepped forward and spoke with slow and careful words. "I am King William of Mead and friend of Alwyn of Newry. We met awhile back when I sought a special oat here in this land to store, and later when they had grown enough, feed the baby unicorns I came upon with the oat from their own land. Alwyn was at the same time seeking the missing pair. We met at Heartmorland and before you dress me down for having Elaine and Enos in my possession, I tell you it was their desire to be with me, for they were near starvation, and I had the solution to end their hunger and sorrow."

King William retold his accounting of his first meeting with the baby unicorns. Then he said, "If you do not mind, Alwyn, I would like to see the place of Darrius's downfall. Since all of you are here, I believe another set of eyes and opinions would be beneficial in regards to solving this horrible crime."

"We will go with you, Alwyn, William." Egwin nodded. "But we must be quick about it. Linden and I have other matters to attend to and supplies to gather."

"As you wish," Alwyn said. The elves and the king went in search of the place where Darrius was found, and they spoke with one another in a more civil tongue.

King William rose from his crouching position and looked at the elves. When he spoke, it was with certainty that he came to his conclusion.

"Darrius was struck by lightning, Alwyn. I have removed a portion of the growing ivy and grass here."

They looked at the ground and agreed it showed a long path of dark burned vegetation beneath it.

William continued, "If you look here at this tree," once again he removed the clinging vines and rubbed off the moss, "it tells me Darrius flew in the air from that position at the far end of this clearing and hit this tree with a great deal of force. From the description of his body given to me, I believe he was already dead when he hit it."

"I cannot believe I missed this." Alwyn spoke with surprise. "I promise I did not see signs of this kind of destruction, this burning."

Again King William spoke. "Let us walk further to find the place of his fight."

After walking several yards they reached the place believed to be the beginning of the sword fight, and William shook his head back and forth.

"How is it possible that Darrius was thrown such a distance?" He was interrupted from speaking more when Egwin pushed free of a dense meadow and said, "Alwyn, Darrius was gathering liquid rubber. His barrel is just over here."

They followed Egwin to the barrel. Alwyn's tears could not be controlled and his temper rose.

"My father was killed for this rubber!" he shouted.

Linden went back to the boat and gathered the wine pouches that were filled with an old elven recipe. It was strong with a bold flavor particularly enjoyed by most elves. He handed each one a pouch, sat down next to King William on the large fallen tree, and drank a goodly portion of his own before he spoke.

"King William, can you tell who did this? Are there clues as to the thing that did this? I say thing because it must be a creature, not an elf, fairy, fey or... Well maybe it was." He did not want to say human, but William said it for him.

"Human, Linden?"

"Sorry, but yes, human."

"I seriously doubt the poor elf was killed for rubber sap, but if there are other clues they may have been washed away from the recent rain." Turning to face Alwyn, King William spoke in a quiet tone. "I am sorry, Alwyn. I hoped to be of more assistance to you. I am heavy of heart knowing of your loss."

Egwin and Linden stood. "We must be on our way, Alwyn. We have many things to gather before we head back. We are sorry that your sorrow has resurfaced and your exploration was for naught." Egwin finished then nodded to Linden. They left King William and Alwyn and headed out to gather their supplies.

After long moments of silence, Alwyn said, "I must gather some clams, William, least Willa be suspicious of my long absence."

"I need to be on my way as well," the king said. "I will go on from here and keep searching for clues, Alwyn." Alwyn nodded his head in agreement.

"Before I go, I wanted to give this to you. I made it myself. Perhaps it will give you a little comfort when you look on it."

King William reached into a pocket of his cloak and removed the hand-carved wooden likenesses of the Elaine and Enos.

"William, this is truly exceptional. You carved this?"

Yes, but if you tell anyone, I will make you very sorry, Alwyn."

Despite his sorrow, Alwyn smiled. "Thank you, William. It is our law that when a gift is given one must be given in return." He rose and removed his jeweled knife and handed it to the king.

"Alwyn, this is a priceless knife. I cannot take this. Do you not have a rock or shell handy?" William asked.

Alwyn burst out laughing despite himself. "Come sit a moment, William." Alwyn pulled a small piece of parchment and a writing implement from a pouch clasped at his waist that he kept for scribbling down his thoughts. William remained standing and waited patiently until Alwyn was finished with his writing.

"Since you are not of a mind to accept my knife, I have decided to give you this secret recipe for the brewing of a favorite elven beer. We call it Gwynness, and it is very strong and full bodied. Follow these instructions to the letter and you will not be disappointed with the results. Do not tell anyone where you obtained this, and I will not confess I gave it to a human. Otherwise, we could both be in a bit of a mess, if you get my meaning."

Alwyn placed the parchment in William's hand and grasped his forearm in a stronghold.

"Thank you for your help, William." William nodded, and Alwyn headed for the ocean's end in search of clams for dinner.

"You think you can get away from me you empty box of nothing?" Mawrthlyn mumbled as he ate one of the rabbits left roasting on the fire. When he finished, he threw the bones behind him, stood, and started to yell for the fey when he realized he did not know the fool's name. Speaking to himself he said, "I will torture him before I kill him for trying to flee. It is his own fault for being so slow and clumsy that I must resort to beating him. A worthless fey if I ever saw one.

"And where is that female human, Agnes, anyway? I spent many long nights training her, and what is my thanks, my reward? I will seek her out after my business with Renewal, and then I will kill her for leaving me alone to be torched like a bonfire by those half-wit elves who think they can remove me from existence!" Mawrthlyn roared his last words, and a nearby screech owl kept its silence. Twisting its head around, it dare not look at the dark figure.

He pounded his feet in anger as he walked about in the dark forest seeking the fey and the Suddeth Spider. He needed the spider's web to sew his wounds together and the fey to accomplish the task. His magic kept his wounds from running his blood out, but he was tired and his magic ebbed and flowed like the tide the more he walked.

"Ah, there you are little spider." Mawrthlyn bent down and retrieved a stick. When he slowly approached the spider, she stood up straight and at the ready to spew her venom at the approach of the stick.

"Shhh, little spider. I only need your web to wind around this stick. You can make another. Do not fear, I will not harm you."

The spider retreated into the opening of a dead palm tree abandoned by a family of birds months ago. It protected the spider well enough, and she nodded her head to Mawrthlyn to begin the winding.

# Chapter Thirteen

Elaine and Enos gently lowered themselves to the ground and nodded as Lutherian and Huw flitted off of them.

"Thank you for your swiftness in coming to this cave entrance," Lutherian said with sincerity and patted them one at a time.

Huw also thanked the unicorns and nodded his head in homage. Although the feys understood the unicorns could speak if they wished to, it was still a shock to hear their music-like voices in unison.

"You are most welcome, Luther, Huw. Please be careful and understand when Meirionwen gains her feet she will still be in a weakened state. You may place her upon one of our backs, and we can fly to the secret garden in all haste. We know well the butterfly's plight in their journey, because we spoke to them before they left. However, we were not aware until just recently about the damage to plants, flowers, bushes, trees, herbs, and fields that sprout hay, wheat, rye, and rice. Our own land is not affected in this way."

Lutherian nodded his understanding and he commanded, "Thirteen torches I call, come forth!"

As they each came forward, a torch followed behind Kim, Glenlillian, Huw, Lutherian, and the nine fairy sisters as they quietly walked into the cave at Bardfey Island and into the unknown.

Merddlyn stood next to the crystal case Meirionwen was locked in. It had taken him the majority of the afternoon to find her. When the first layers of the soft sandstone fell away from the granite rock upon Merddlyn's command, he spotted a tiny glow of amber crystal glimmering in the dancing flames of a floating torch. When the last of the sandstone came away from the tomb, Merddlyn found whom he sought. He did not expect the sadness that overwhelmed him, for clearly visible was the look of pain frozen upon Meirionwen's face. The amber crystal obscured her paleness, and the wizard felt a deep regret when he realized she was hidden just steps away from him after he awoke from his own sleep.

He was thinking only of himself at the time of her wounding, of his own tiredness and desire to be alone. His selfishness obscured those moments alerting him to Meirionwen's impending danger. All he could think about was getting to the caves at Bardfey. Just moments after he left for the island, she had been sliced by a blade from the two remaining knights still fighting, unaware that the war was over.

Hidden by a cloak of invisibility, the fairy went unseen as she glided between them. The accident left her so deeply wounded that she could barely think, let alone find the strength to encase herself. How could he not know she was seeking him those many years ago? Why did he not look behind him for just a moment? He would have seen her seeking him. Would Glenlillian forgive him if they could not save Meirionwen, Great Diamond Fairy?

He thought of releasing her himself before the others arrived, but he did not have much of a healing hand and knew she would bleed to death in his clumsy attempts to fix her. He stopped berating himself, for it would not undo the past. The glow of the approaching torches made Merddlyn turn toward the entrance. He waited patiently for the fairies and feys to reach him.

King William walked to his horse and decided to head home. The thunder in the distance told him he had little time before the storm would arrive, so he kicked his horse into a run. The cold late afternoon air was not good for him, and he hunched down into his cloak, hoping his horse could outrun the rain. He had gotten as far as a trading post located just beyond Polnairs Retreat when the deluge came down in pelting sheets. His only option was to stop there and wait inside until the storm passed. With difficulty, he tied his horse to a latching pole and quickly entered the trading post.

Several men were there sitting at the available tables recently set up by the owner. They were enjoying mead mixed with wine and taking turns telling tall tales about dragons.

King William shook the rain off his cloak and placed it on a wooden peg next to one of many near the entrance. He walked to the long bar table, behind which stood Mr. Johansson. He was pouring himself a tall mug of something steaming hot, and he spoke to the merchant.

"I do not suppose you would happen to have another tall mug of whatever that is for a cold wet stranger to enjoy this thunderous and rainy day?" William asked.

"Indeed I do, my good man. Please, have a seat at the fire and warm yourself. I will join you straightaway."

William nodded and sought the welcoming warmth of the fire.

The hot wine spilled slightly as Mr. Johansson approached the hearth chairs. After handing one to King William, he sat down and struck up a conversation.

"My wife, Meredith, may her soul be at rest, loved to sit here. She said the fire made her hands work swiftly while she sewed up my torn shirts and aprons. That the warmth comforted her aching bones, and the crackling sound of the burning wood was magical. I can still recall the sound of her beautiful voice humming as she worked."

William saw the sadness in the man's eyes, and he introduced himself.

"My name is William, and I was heading home before the heavens opened up and spit on me."

Mr. Johansson roared with laughter, and the others joined in repeating nearly the same story of not wishing to be caught in the approaching storm. William sipped his hot wine and nodded in appreciation that he was not the only fool out in that stormy weather. Suddenly, Mr. Johansson jumped up from his seat, bowed down, and spoke in a breathless whisper. "Forgive me, King William. I did not recognize you at first." The others, upon hearing Mr. Johansson's words, bowed as the owner did and stammered their apologies while they waited for the king to acknowledge them.

"Please just call me William. I am not at the castle, nor do I wish for anyone here to treat me any differently than if I were an ordinary goods-seeking merchant."

A stiff cold wind blew in as the front door was again opened, and another man walked in. Wet and thirsty, Sir Jahaziel shook his cloak, hung it on an available peg, and walked to the long table. Turning at the sound of a familiar voice, he smiled and roared with laughter.

"King William! You sure are a sight for sore eyes."

With a sound slap on Jahaziel's back, King William laughed out loud and asked, "What brings you here, Sir Jahaziel?"

"Women's tasks I am afraid." He turned to Mr. Johansson and said, "Paul, do you still have those lavender hair ribbons from Southland?"

"I do indeed, Sir Jahaziel. Let me fetch them for you. How many do you need?"

"Wait. Before you go digging around in your wooden boxes, how about pouring me some hot wine as well?"

"Yes, of course. Straightaway."

William chuckled at Paul's words and spoke his question. "Did my cousin send you on this women's errand, Jahaziel?"

"Sire, it was Queen Joyce, Siomara, Princess Teri, Agnes, several women servants, and a little girl I do not know."

"Agnes? Did you say Agnes?" William asked.

"'Tis a long story, Sire, and I need my wine before the telling," Jahaziel uttered.

William pointed to the seats near the fire and sat back down on the chair he recently occupied. Jahaziel sat in the other.

Before he could speak, Jahaziel shouted to Paul, "I think you should make this a men's club, Paul, and no women allowed!"

The sound of clinking mugs and "Here, here," bounced around the trading post hut.

As the rain blew and wind howled all the louder, Jahaziel quietly told King William everything he knew about the sad tale of Agnes. He wanted to make sure no other ears could hear their conversation, so he leaned in closer to the king and spoke in a weary voice.

"Sire, I was as shocked as you when I was told Agnes had returned to Fitzhuwlyn. However, she seems to be settling in. She was asked to be an attendant at Princess Teri and Myles's wedding."

He did not mention the fact that he was her escort when he answered King William's question of it being a nice affair.

"Well, I think we should ride back together once this rain stops and you have gathered the requested ribbons. What say you, Jahaziel? Would you like a bit of company on the ride back?"

"I would be most grateful for it, Sire. It will be a slow ride back, but I am at ease knowing the moon will soon rise to offer us enough light that we may return safely."

Mawrthlyn looked everywhere for the fey. He went into a rage when he realized he had escaped. His thoughts wandered in and out as the ragging headache pounded his brain. His own anger was sucking the life out of him, and he decided once again to rest. After walking for what seemed many miles, he came upon a small cave. It was dry and not an unpleasant place. With plenty of room for his long legs, he stretched out, lowered the hood of his cape over his eyes, and fell into a deep sleep.

His dream was disturbing, and his eyes flitted back and forth under their lids. He was arguing with Renewal, and she was dressing him down with harsh words. Finally, the blackness came to him, and he was being reinvigorated, restored, and strengthened by it.

Suddenly, the sound of power began to float among the trees. A power long lost that had lain trapped and dormant until now. Mawrthlyn woke with a start. He needed to get to Renewal before the power was unleashed. He realized that a great power was unfolding at the approach of night, and he wanted to possess it. With all of his being, he desired it.

Mawrthlyn slowly walked within the dense forest that would eventually lead to a hidden path he and his brother created when they were very young wizards. Staying within the shadows, he moved with methodical intent on reaching the cave and Renewal as quickly as he was able, but the pain was still with him and his burns throbbed.

He mumbled to himself, "The first thing I will demand, no, no, gently persuade Renewal to do is heal my remaining wounds. This pain distracts me, and I cannot think clearly."

He was not aware that the oozing darkness still followed in his wake. Each area Mawrthlyn walked past, the oozing darkness slowly shriveled the greenery behind him. And like a lake that begins to freeze in the cold winter air, the forest crackled with the sound of death.

Mirrorme saw the shadow as it walked past her. She concentrated with great intent to slow her breathing down as she stood in the shadows not moving, waiting, and hiding behind the large pine. She watched in horror as the dying forest crumpled in the wake of the shadow. Suddenly, Mawrthlyn stopped and turned around. Instinct told him he was being watched. Mirrorme sucked in her breath and held it.

She could hold her breath for long moments when she remembered the sea.

The only sounds Mawrthlyn heard were the brittle leaves as they danced in circles close to the ground when a chilling breeze swept by them. Mawrthlyn continued on his journey and disappeared into the shadows once again.

Mirrorme sat down on the ground hard and took in deep breaths, gulping in the air as quickly as she could. *I will not cry,* she told herself. As her breathing slowed she called to Kim Gold Fairy to be watchful of the approaching darkness.

"Merddlyn, how long have you been waiting?" Huw asked as he entered the huge area of the cave.

"Not long. I have been contemplating how we can release Meirionwen quickly, attend her wounds, and give her a little strength before you entered. She will be in shock, and we have little time to do this."

Glenlillian and the others came forward. She looked at her mother and could not help her tears.

Lutherian hugged her and asked, "Can you do this, Glen? Can you set your feelings aside and focus on the task at hand?"

"Of course. I just need a moment to gather my thoughts."

Red Fairy flitted forward, and her torch followed behind. It hovered with quaking flame at the sight of Meirionwen frozen in the crystal.

"It will be Okay, torch. Do not be frightened. Go, seek another torch for Meirionwen. She will need its light to see and its warmth."

The torch quickly left, and Red Fairy turned to the group and spoke with strange authority.

"You must listen to me. We need to practice removing Meirionwen from her tomb before we actually do it. This must be done in quick, precisely gauged measures. One mistake or misstep will be our loss of her. Do you all understand?"

Merddlyn nodded his head and asked, "What do you wish us to do, Red?"

Just then Red Fairy's torch came in with another torch. Addressing them she said, "Both of you hover on each side of the crystal tomb. Rise up, yes, a little more. Good. Stay," she commanded. Addressing everyone once again, she spoke with careful words as she turned to Merddlyn.

"First of all, do you know how to open the crystal, Merddlyn?"

Before he spoke, another answered Red Fairy's question.

"I can open her tomb."

Everyone looked at Huw and stared in shock. Before they could say a word, he called his harp forward. "Harp, come."

It quickly did Huw's bidding and gently placed itself in front of him. Satisfied the harp did not make a sound, Huw lowered himself and then sat down upon a large rock. The harp followed him and settled itself between Huw's legs.

"This harp is made with a special blend of magic. It has many abilities when played in a certain order. It can open Meirionwen's tomb without harm to her." Huw now addressed the harp with stern words. "You will not play until I tell you to. I will pretend to stroke your strings but do not play. We are pretending to play. Do you understand?"

The sound of the B flat string saying yes memorized everyone, and a quiet stillness settled into the cave. Red Fairy snapped out of her brain pause and began to assemble everyone in the order in which they needed to participate in the monumental task.

"Purple, did you bring the woven Talasi plant mat?"

"Yes, yes. Here it is, Red."

"Place it at the base of the crystal." Red Fairy spoke in rushed words as Purple Fairy quickly laid the mat and flitted back to her place among the assembled.

"Orange. I need you to stand guard outside of this cave entrance and make it invisible. We cannot risk being interrupted by anyone or anything. Do you understand? You can do it, Orange. You have the strength."

Orange Fairy nodded and went to the cave entrance. Rising up, she spread her wings, and then threw them forward. A strong wind blew as the cave entrance disappeared from view along with her. Satisfied they would not be discovered by anyone or anything, Red Fairy continued giving orders.

"Purple, I need you to gather lightning in to your hands and hold it there. Do not look at me as if I do not know what I speak of. I have seen you practicing with it," Red Fairy said.

Purple Fairy nodded, then closed her eyes and commanded a small bolt of lightning forward. The cracking sound surprised everyone, and Purple Fairy quickly pulled it into a ball and closed her hands around it, addressing her sister as she did so. "I can hold it as long as you wish me to, Red."

"Good. When I give you the signal, hit Meirionwen in the heart with the lightning ball. This will shock her awake.

"Green, have you mixed the potion Meiri needs to drink so she may quickly gain her strength?" A nod was her answer.

"Blue, I need you to begin singing the healing song. Quietly, please. Pink, we will need to put out the torches' flames, except for the two commanded to hover near Meiri. The light from your wings is the only light we will need until we leave this cave.

"Yellow, think positive, kind thoughts and concentrate. Do not let your mind wander. Brown, I need you and Merddlyn to stand at the ready if anything should start falling apart. There is much power in the cave with us all assembled here. White, I need you to go through the wrinkle and warn us of any impending trouble.

"Mother, Grandmother, the moment Meirionwen falls from the crystal, start sewing up her wound. It might be quicker if you each start at opposites ends. Then quickly wrap the wound binding cloth around her leg."

"We know our job, Red," Kim said smiling.

The last of her commands were addressed to Lutherian.

"Grandfather, when Meirionwen comes away from the crystal, hold her tightly to you until Grandmother and Mother finish sewing and binding her wound. Once she is strong enough to travel, place her on one of the unicorns and ride

138

with her. After all we have done, I do not wish her to fall off the horse and break her neck. Huw can ride the other unicorn and White and Mother will send the rest of us to the gardens. We will wait for you there." Red Fairy ended her words and took a moment to relax before the practice run.

King Crawford and Jahaziel were on their way to the bailey to gather up the newly knighted men for a well-needed practice. Too much overindulgence of food and wine at the wedding had left the guards lazy and unwilling to participate in the regular routine of weapons practice and repair, hand combat, and riding. As the evening approached, halfway across the yard the first rumblings of the ground began. It shook for several moments, and three servants ran from the castle screaming for the king. A large oak was suddenly ripped from the ground by its roots; and with horrendous sound, it fell near the stables.

Agnes was just approaching the meadow with the intent to gather the only remaining wildflowers close to the border of Fitzhuwlyn Castle when the ground split open in front of her. She nearly lost her balance, pitching forward then backward. Deciding on her best course of action to prevent from tumbling into the widening crevasse, she quickly sat down on the grass and waited for the shaking to stop. Her head felt woozy, and a sickness settled in her stomach. Looking around, Agnes spotted the king and Jahaziel walking toward her, and she jumped up and ran quickly, closing the distance between them. She flung herself into Jahaziel arms; and in a moment of weakness, he held her tightly to him. Agnes was shaking from fear. She and the wide cracks that suddenly appeared in the ground in front of them stunned Jahaziel.

# Chapter Fourteen

The king walked to Jahaziel and Agnes and spoke. "The earth quakes as if a thousand men on horses have rushed here in a stampede and suddenly stopped. How is this possible, Jahaziel? Have you ever heard or seen such a thing?"

"No, Sire. I have not." Then he looked at Agnes, still in Jahaziel's embrace, and he tried very hard not to smile. "Are you all right, Agnes? Are you hurt?"

"No, Sire." Separating herself from Jahaziel, she looked at him a moment and then walked toward the castle saying, "I should check inside to be sure no one is hurt."

Then she ran as if the devil himself was after her.

When Jahaziel looked at Crawford, he hollered, "Do not say it, Sire. Do not."

"I will keep my own counsel for the moment. Let us walk around and see if there is more damage than what is here."

Jahaziel followed his king and walked to the stables where the horses were still baying in fear. Several stable men were desperately trying to calm the frightened horses, and the king and Jahaziel joined them in the struggle.

When Agnes entered the kitchen, nearly every pot and pan was on the floor along with all the crockery Maggie prided herself on keeping clean and neatly aligned on the open shelving near a wall. The shelf above the kitchen fireplace was also emptied of its many candles. Agnes stepped over the mess and went to Maggie. She was weeping into her apron with her back to the hearth wall. When she spotted Agnes, she ran to her, knocking the cluttered mess everywhere. Agnes patted her on the shoulder and spoke quietly.

"Maggie, it will be Okay. Let us clean up this mess before the queen sees it, all right?"

All Maggie could do was nod her head yes, but she did not move from Agnes's side.

"Do you know where Merddlyn is, Egwin?" Farian questioned.

"He should be along shortly. Do you have everything we need for the journey, Linden?"

"Yes. I think we should tell our fathers we are leaving and let them be at the ready for trouble that may come this way," Linden said.

Farian began to laugh and said, "Did you see the looks on their faces when Merddlyn reinstated them as Destroyers of Darkness. I did not know my father could yell so loud. I believe there was not a dry eye in the clubhouse."

They walked out to meet up with the wizard.

Merddlyn was waiting for the Destroyers of Darkness at Egwin's home. His mind was still reeling from the rescue and healing of Meirionwen. With the speed of a well-trained army, the fairies and feys had completed the difficult task in a blinding dance of awesome wonder.

He recalled his conversation with Kim and her insistence on coming with him. His emphatic no upset her, and she left him alone for a moment to wallow in his stubbornness.

"Kim, I am no longer needed here. I am to meet up with Linden, Farian, and Egwin at Egwin's home. It is time the Destroyers of Darkness and I search for my brother. I fear time is slipping away, and he will obtain all he desires."

"Wait. I am going with you. I am part of this as well. I can jump ahead to locate his whereabouts for you," Kim said.

"You are needed in the garden. You cannot come with me."

"There are too many fairies in that garden as far as I am concerned, and I, for one, am glad the rescue of the Crystal Butterflies is in more capable hands. I can get you to Edwin's quickly, Merddlyn. Let us not waste time discussing this!"

"No! You will not come with me. Besides, I weigh more than all of your daughters, Glenlillian, Luther, Huw and…" Merddlyn started to laugh.

"My powers grow and continue to as we stand here shouting at one another. So do not force me to use them on you!"

In a quieter tone, Merddlyn said, "No, Kim. Please go back to the garden."

He left Kim sputtering utterances he had only heard once spewing from Huw when he observed him unseen as he trained his new guards.

As he headed for Egwin's home, Kim appeared at his side and took his hand in hers. His laughter was uncontrollable, and he spoke with difficulty. "How do Huw and Jahaziel put up with you and all your peculiarities?"

In one fairy moment, they were at Egwin's home.

Maximillian was cowering in a corner of the bed he found himself in when he woke from his sleep. He did not know yet again where he was. He still did not know his name, and he was still in fear of Master. The slow squeak of a door opening had Maximillian covering his body with the blanket that had been neatly folded at the bed's foot.

As the approaching sound of footsteps came closer and closer he screamed, "Please, please, please, do not hurt me. I will do all you ask, just do not hurt me!"

The last of his words fell away in his fit of crying.

Broadwayne and Cassiarian sat in the stools next to the bed, and Cassiarian spoke in a gentle voice.

"Do not be frightened. We will not hurt you. Will you come out from under those covers and speak with us, Max?"

With shaking hands, Maximillian lowered the warm blanket to his chin, and his eyes widened in surprise as he looked at the two feys sitting near him.

"My name is Broadwayne, and this is Cassiarian. Your name is Maximillian, and we have been looking everywhere for you."

"Max, can you sit up? I have brought you some healing broth that was prepared by a Crystal Fairy. Her name is Glenlillian. She, Cass, and I have been very worried ever since you disappeared."

With a shaky voice, Maximillian asked, "How long have I been disappeared?"

"Before we answer your questions, you must eat. Cass here brought you fresh bread to go with that broth, and we have enough for all of us to enjoy."

Broadwayne shoved Cassiarian in friendly banter, and then handed Maximillian his soup and bread. As they ate in silence, a small hint of a smile showed on Maximillian's face as he relaxed for the first time since his awakening.

Meirionwen kissed each unicorn, and then waved as they took flight to answer an unheard call from an unknown source. Meirionwen looked at her daughter with joyful tears in her eyes and spoke with a bit of difficulty. She had not used her vocal cords in so long, she thought she might not ever be able to speak again.

Slowly she began her speech. "I am overjoyed to see all of you, but now is not the time for our visitation and reunion. You must circle me quickly and stay in this position as we glide through the garden."

All the fairies quickly circled Meirionwen and held each other's hands in a tight grip as Meirionwen continued speaking. "Luther, Huw, as we hover over the ground where the crystal seeds sleep, pour a generous amount of Sassafras over this weed-infested ground and within our circle.

"We must all sing the song of healing quietly and repetitively until the flowers bloom to their full and complete state. Once that has been done to my satisfaction, we will all pluck one butterfly at a time from suspension. Our touch will awaken them, and we must hold each one very steady as we sing the birthing song. Once they gain their senses, they will circle around us and immediately begin feeding. These butterflies are the original butterflies that have migrated back to our lands.

"There are seven different species of Crystal Butterflies and seven identical butterflies within each group for a total of forty-nine Crystal Butterflies. When these butterflies eat their fill, they will fly to the next clan, signaling the second group of forty-nine butterflies to this garden to feed. This second group will then follow the path of the first group and feed at each garden. This process is repeated until all seven groups of forty-nine butterflies reach the Clan of Oneth. Oneth has the largest gardens and is quite capable of feeding three hundred and forty-three butterflies. It is imperative that we try and stay ahead of the butterflies as they head for Oneth. When we are finished healing our gardens, I must rest awhile before we tackle the job of healing the other lands.

Glen, I hope you brought a bit more of that healing tea with you. We will all need a cupful after we are finished here."

"Yes, I have plenty to go around, Mother."

Meirionwen took a deep breath and continued.

"Now, here is the difficult part. We must visit each clan garden for an assessment. We will repeat our sequence of flower healing at every clan garden affected by this oozing darkness. If we manage to get ahead of it and no damage is reported or seen, we will throw a cover of protection over those gardens. I will tell you how this is to be done once we arrive at the unaffected areas.

"I understand from Glenlillian that each caretaker will be waiting for our arrival and will join us in the healing process." Turning to her daughter, Meirionwen asked, "Glen, may I have a sip of your healing tea before we begin?"

With a nod of her head and tears in her eyes, Glenlillian poured the tea and handed it to her mother.

Before Meirionwen could utter another word, a rumbling sound was heard coming from underground. Immediately after the rumbling started, the ground shook with such violence that several young sapling trees came away from their planted place, roots and all, and fell to the ground. Several of the fairies barely had enough time to fly out of the way of the falling trees. Everyone started shouting over one another, and Lutherian and Huw bellowed for silence.

"What in all the blazing stars was that?" the fairy sisters said as if one voice spoke.

They were high in the top of an ancient oak tree and did not realize until that moment that they were safe. When Lutherian commanded them to come down, they shook their heads.

"Egwin, take this lasso and tie it around your waist. Take care not to lose it. It took me several sun risings to get it just right. Once we tackle Mawrthlyn, I will bind his hands and feet while you sit on him. No matter what, do not let him up. I have no idea of his strength, so let us assume he can cause irreparable harm to anyone of us at will."

Turning to Kim, Egwin spoke with sternness. "Kim, you must stay ahead of him and report back to us at regular intervals. Do not let him see you, and do not get in his way. Go quickly and tell us where he is."

Kim nodded and then disappeared.

"I am not comfortable with the notion that Kim could be captured by your brother, Merddlyn. Linden, Farian, and I are uneasy about her being here with us." Egwin sighed.

"You told me, did you not, that she was part of this society? Well, now she is doing her part, and, frankly, my worry is that she is not worried. It scares the blazes out of me that she is so nonchalant about Mawrthlyn, but I trust her instincts. Now, show me everything you brought with you. I need to assess your weapons."

Merddlyn held up a large curved blade with a handle large enough for his own grip and asked Linden what it was. His shy response and red face had Merddlyn laughing out loud.

"I made it to cut off his feet if he tries to run from us. One swipe and the deed will be done."

Kim reappeared breathing hard. She needed a moment.

"Mawrthlyn is just crossing the Lembath River. Apparently he fell in because he is soaked from head to foot. He was mumbling words I did not understand. He may need to rest and dry off. This might be the opportunity we need to capture him."

"Then let us go in all haste and stop him before he reaches Karapalis. He has many hiding places there, and I do not know all of them," Merddlyn said.

147

As the sun slowly began to set, the Destroyers of Darkness trudged slowly along the border of Coremerick. It was obvious that the lands were affected by the oozing darkness. Everywhere they looked, dead shriveled vegetation continued to wither and crumple before their very eyes. As they headed in the direction that Kim had spotted Mawrthlyn, they were suspicious that her tracking of Mawrthlyn seemed a bit too easy.

Merddlyn put a finger to his mouth to silence them. He looked directly at Kim and motioned her to go forward to seek Mawrthlyn once again.

Carefully, Kim floated ahead, hiding between the trees. Leaves were falling like snowflakes as the withering of the trees began. Kim did not see him, but she smelled him. The dampness of his cloak and clothing was strong, and she slowly made her way back to the elves and Merddlyn.

"I believe he is in that cave just a few yards from here. I hear no movement, but I can smell his damp clothing."

Merddlyn nodded to Farian, Egwin, and Linden. They slowly removed the weapons from their leather pouches and walked in a line toward the cave.

One at a time, with quiet steps, they entered with caution. Kim was commanded to stay outside and to be cautious and mindful of any danger that might approach. Merddlyn stood in front of Mawrthlyn's discarded cloak lying on the cave floor, and he realized too late that it was a trap. Kim's sudden scream caused them to swiftly turn around, and they ran toward the entrance of the cave.

Mawrthlyn had just enough time to seal them inside. With a raised hand, he dropped a large boulder down in front of the opening. He knew he was being spied on by a fairy, and he flew at Kim with great speed. After several attempts, he managed to grab her by an arm but she quickly slid free of his grasp and disappeared from his sight.

His bellow shook the remaining leaves from the trees nearest him, and Mawrthlyn ran off in a rage. He could not believe they had a powerful fairy with them. The next time he got a grip on her she would not break free of him. He vowed it. Then he would kill her and leave her body hanging from a dead tree where he knew the Destroyers of Darkness would come upon her. It would serve as a warning for them to stop tracking him.

Kim was still shaking and thanked the heavens no bonding with Mawrthlyn took place, which confirmed what Egwin had surmised: only acts of kindness can bond a fairy to another species. Mirrorme suddenly appeared next to Kim and spoke quickly.

*I saw the danger of the dark one coming for you. I was walking in this area and heard your scream. I do not understand why this darkened figure comes for you, but I know where it has gone, Kim. I could feel its anger as it quickly passed me, and I believe the anger makes it careless. I can track it for you. It is not safe for you now that it has touched you. Go. I will follow that dark thing.*

Kim hugged Mirrorme, and then swiftly went to the cave to help Merddlyn remove the boulder from its entrance. Only when they were released would she be able to breathe a sigh of relief.

Jahaziel and King Crawford saw King William coming fast. His horse had sweat dripping from it; and when he quickly pulled on the reigns to stop it, the horse skidded several feet. William jumped from the saddle and rushed to the king and knight.

"Did you feel the ground shaking, Crawford?" He nodded to Jahaziel and waited for Crawford to answer him.

"Yes, and there are fissures so deep I can see the ocean slowly seeping up. I gauge two days from now we will have a few long but narrow waterways. They have appeared in several places along the border of North/Southland and here. Something untoward is happening, and I do not know what can be done to stop it. What about Mead, William?"

"No fissures, just a lot of ground shaking. I do believe I lost every pottery plate I own."

"Well, we seem to have a few wine cups still in tack. Come, let us seek a good brew and discuss this happening."

William smiled at the suggestion of a cup of brew, and his thoughts went to the recipe Alwyn had given him. He started a mental list of all the things he would need to start the process of brewing the Gwynness.

As they sat at the long table in the reception hall, wine was served, and Queen Joyce and Agnes joined them.

William smiled at his cousin and questioned her. "Where are Myles and Teri?"

"They have gone on an after-wedding journey to see the waterfalls of Middle/Southland. From there they plan on boating down the river close to Dunbrietown near Lenox. After a day or two there, they will head back."

"I doubt they have experienced this ground shaking so far south. I truly hope it is over and that we will be left in peace, not in pieces," William quipped.

Joyce caught a glimpse of Agnes smiling at Jahaziel, and she closed her eyes in thankful wonder.

When William questioned her smile, she quickly said, "I am smiling because you have come for dinner."

As the plates and wine cups were being cleared away, Agnes walked to where Jahaziel was seated at the table.

"Can I get you anything else from the kitchen while I am up, Jahaziel?"

"Perhaps a bit of your company. Will you sit with me, Agnes?"

"Yes, of course." When she sat down upon the stool that he pulled out for her, Jahaziel looked directly into her eyes.

"I did not realize until now that your eyes are not blue but a light shade of purple. A rare color to be sure."

His smile was lovely, and Agnes could not help smiling in return.

While they spoke to one another in quiet conversation, they were not aware everyone else had left the table.

# Chapter Fifteen

The Crystal Butterflies were feeding happily upon the sparkling crystal flowers. The soft sound emitting from their clicking wings had Lutherian, Huw, and all the fairies smiling in appreciation and wonder.

Meirionwen floated next to Lutherian and, speaking in whispered words, said, "It is good to hear this sound again. It has been many years since I first caught a glimpse of their first flight and feeding, and do not dare ask my age, Luther." He laughed, and she continued to smile as they hovered quietly near the butterflies.

Huw coughed, breaking the silence. "We need to get ahead of their feeding and follow their flight plan, Luther. Are you rested enough to continue on to the next stop at Coremerick, Meirionwen?"

"Yes, thank you, Huw. We should get moving and be prepared for anything. I, for one, do not like surprises."

As they headed for Coremerick, they glided together in tight formation. The fairy sisters could not stop touching Meirionwen, and she had a difficult time knowing they were all Kim and Huw's babies all grown up, strong, and ready for many adventures of their own. When Glenlillian glided close to her she asked, "Mother. Do you know why the ground shakes?"

"Yes." Glenlillian waited for the answer, but it did not come, so she questioned Meirionwen again.

"All right. If you will not tell me, will you at least tell Luther?"

"No, Glen, not just yet. Our only focus at this moment must be the healing of all the gardens so the butterflies may continue on their flight path. I will not let the portents of doom come upon this land or us now that I am released from the crystal. But be assured of this, we are doing everything that needs to be done. We can deal with this destructive darkness. As all things begin to unfold, circumstance and fate will lead us to one point and one end."

Glenlillian did not understand her mother's words, so she looked ahead as the clan approached Coremerick.

They should not have been surprised but they were. The destruction of the gardens at Coremerick was by far worse than Phenloris. They stared with wide-open eyes and slowly lowered themselves to the ground.

The garden caretaker, a second-generation fairy, was named after the first caretaker and she was the exact image of her mother. Her youthful appearance did not reveal her true age to the group. The first Aleese had lived long enough to instruct her daughter on the care of the butterflies, and when the end of her time was approaching, she went over all the instructions with her daughter once again. When she was satisfied with Aleese's promise to care for the garden and butterflies, she went on to the place all fairies finally go, a world beyond this world, to join her family forever.

Aleese approached the clan with caution, and all could see the tears in her eyes. Glenlillian and Meirionwen went immediately to her.

"Aleese, do not distress yourself. None of this destruction you see before you is your fault," Glenlillian stated.

It was clear to both Meirionwen and Glenlillian that Aleese was frightened. She gulped in air in an effort to speak, but she could not.

Glenlillian turned to Red Fairy and said in a whisper, "Could you please bring me a little of the healing tea, Red?" Red Fairy returned quickly with the tea, and Meirionwen coaxed Aleese to drink.

She closed her eyes and let the tea comfort her. Moments later she spoke. "I saw what did this. It was a tall, dark, cloaked figure that walked quickly past this area in anger. It was in a great hurry and did not see me bending down as I tended the garden. When it continued on its journey, the blackness followed behind it. Then everything began to wither. In the quickest of moments, all the beautiful crystal flowers fell to the ground with a crackling sound, and I could do nothing to fix the destruction."

Meirionwen hugged her and said, "Aleese, with your help we can undo all the damage. Take a bit more tea, and then we will begin when you are ready."

Mirrorme was acting very shy in Merddlyn's company. Her cheeks were streaked in a light shade of pink, and she had a little sparkle to her eyes. When Kim saw her smiling, she knew Mirrorme was clearly smitten. Then she introduced her to the wizard.

154

"Mirrorme, this is Merddlyn. Merddlyn, this is Mirrorme. She is a friend to me and my family."

Mirrorme lowered her eyes in shyness, and she blushed all the more from Kim's kind words.

"I am pleased to meet you, Mirrorme." He held out his hand, took hers into his, and he lowered his face to her fingers and kissed them. Kim had a look of surprise on her face, for she heard an amazing sound. Mirrorme clearly giggled, and her face turned a deep shade of red. Kim raised her eyes to the sky and shook her head slightly. Next Kim introduced her to Egwin, Linden, and Farian.

"Meme has agreed to help us. Her unique gift of mind speak can warn me of danger in the quickness of a single moment. She also can camouflage herself to blend in with her surroundings, as well as track prey with a stealthy intent. I have just told Meme about Mawrthlyn, and she has agreed to continue to track him since I am now useless to you in that regard.

"You are a land mermaid, I understand." Merddlyn addressed Mirrorme again.

Kim was confused by his demeanor and spoke a little harsher than she had intended. "Can you stop flirting with Meme for one moment, Merddlyn? We need to leave this moment. Meme, please go ahead again and see if you can find Mawrthlyn."

Mirrorme raised her head, focused her eyes in a squint, and nodded. As she ran from their meeting with great speed, no sound followed her.

"We should have asked her to come at the start, Kim," Egwin stated. Grunts of agreement came from the elves and Merddlyn. Kim glided ahead of the group in quiet solitude.

After several long moments passed, Mirrorme's voice drifted to her and Kim stopped in midair.

*Oh, Kim. The dark wizard has passed by Karapalis and is reaching Llanider. The destruction is getting worse and spreading far and wide. We must stop him. All the woodland creatures will die of starvation, and the trees have begun to wither.*

Kim asked Mirrorme if she could see Mawrthlyn.

*Yes. He is sitting on a fallen tree in a narrow glen eating something disgusting. He has not discovered me because I have covered my scent with moss, mud, and—well, you do not want to know what else I have slathered on my cape.*

Mirrorme could hear Kim laughing. She asked her to stay put until she spoke with Merddlyn, Linden, Farian, and Egwin on what course of action they should take next.

"What do you mean you must leave? Where are you going, and when do you suppose you will return, Kim?" Merddlyn bellowed.

"The destruction your brother has caused is getting worse. Meme has told me he rests in a glen near Llanider. Do not go there until I get back. I will only be a moment. I need to tell my mother where he is and describe the desolation he is leaving in his wake." Then she was gone from his sight.

Mirrorme stayed close to the dark one, while her mind went to the face of the kindly wizard. A sudden realization came to her, and she was certain they were twins. She knew well the nature of humans and twins. If separated, they somehow knew where each twin was; and if one twin was confronted with danger, much like Mirrorme had been, the other twin knew instantly and could communicate without words. She wondered how they became mind separated. What trauma had caused it? She snapped out of her thoughts when she heard Mawrthlyn moving about. She cautiously walked behind him and could hear his mumblings.

"If they think they can bind me again, they have another thing coming. I need to lay a trap. I need to kill them all so that I may travel in peace. Peace. What peace there will be at our reunion at Oneth. What great joy will be had by us at our meeting. Wait my dear, be patient. I will be with you soon."

Mirrorme's eyes rose in curiosity, and she spoke to herself. *What was he mumbling about? Who is she? Where in Oneth was she?* Mirrorme did not realize tears were running down her face, and her thought was a sorrowful one indeed. *He is insane, and that is why he and Merddlyn are mind separated.* She continued on behind him and listened to more of his mumblings that no longer made sense. Mawrthlyn was so into his own head, he was not aware he was being followed.

In one fairy moment, Kim appeared before her mother and grandmother. They looked up from their task of mixing more healing Sassafras and blinked at Kim in surprise.

Kim spoke in a rush. "I do not have time to explain my sudden appearance, but you need to know the oozing darkness has caused more damage then we could have imagined. You will need more Sassafras than what you have brought with you. After you have righted the gardens, you must all hover in a wide straight line and float slowly across the damaged areas of land, pouring the Sassafras as you go. Stay well behind." Kim took a chance and said his name, "Mawrthlyn. He is dangerous and heads for Oneth. He is determined to reach the shoreline. I do not know why he goes there but, he has a sinister purpose to be sure."

Glenlillian was now hovering in front of Kim. "Mawrthlyn?" she stammered.

"Yes, Mother. Mawrthlyn has done all of this and more."

Meirionwen, Great Diamond Fairy floated forward and spoke with authority. "If we stay on this path, we would eventually make our way to Oneth." Meirionwen paused a moment to gather her thoughts, and then continued speaking. "Ever since we arrived here at Coremerick, I have heard a voice calling to me. We are all being summoned to the cave at Oneth by the ancient one. She is the one who has been speaking to your daughters, Kim, and to the others. She is bringing a great change to our land, and we must meet her as quickly as possible. I cannot believe Mawrthlyn has caused this deliberate destruction. "It is apparent to me now that his plan was to keep all of us so busy with righting the gardens and lands that we would not focus on who or what started all this. We must help the Destroyers of Darkness stop him before he reaches Oneth."

Meirionwen turned to Kim. "Go back to Merddlyn and tell him if he can bind his brother, Glenlillian and I can crystal encase him."

"Grandmother, how do you know about the Destroyers of Darkness?" Kim asked.

"I am absorbing information at this very moment. It has taken me awhile to sort through what I know from what I suppose, and it is best for everyone—"

Glenlillian interrupted her. "Mother, do you speak of Renewal? Is Mawrthlyn trying to reach Renewal?"

Meirionwen was surprised at her words. "Yes. How do you know of Renewal? Has she spoken to you, Glen?"

Glenlillian answered with great sadness in her voice, and it pained her heart to remember her mother's encasement. "When I found you locked in the crystal those many years ago, I tried to release you. My puny efforts did not work, and I fell asleep at the base of the crystal tomb in sorrow. Just before I awoke, I heard her voice in my dream." Glenlillian went to that place in her mind and repeated Renewal's words to her.

*"Shhh. Hush, little one. Do not be so sorrowful. I make a promise to you this day that you will see your mother again. In this life, you will be reunited. I am Renewal of Oneth, and I tell you this truth. Be patient and mindful of your duties from this moment on. You will grow with grace and dignity and become a great fairy. Many will seek your counsel and be healed by your hand. Wake now, Glenlillian of the Clan Phenloris. Sweetling, wake."*

Lutherian floated to the three fairies he loved more than his own life and apologized for snooping on their conversation. But he and Huw heard every word.

"We must make a plan to head off Mawrthlyn, Kim. Your fairies can handle the task of righting these gardens. Huw, can you play your harp to send a message to Cassiarian to bring more Sassafras?"

"Yes. I will do this straightaway Luther." Huw flew to his harp and began to play the request.

"Glen, you, Meirionwen, Huw, and I will go straight to Dolbatheryn to try and head him off. We can plan what to do on our way there. Kim, go back to the Destroyers of Darkness and tell them to meet us at Dolbatheryn. They will need to try and get ahead of Mawrthlyn without being seen or heard. Meirionwen, can you send word upon the wind to all the fairy caretakers to leave their gardens? It is for their own safety."

Meirionwen nodded and with whispered words sent the message. Lutherian continued, "If Mawrthlyn gets wind of where we are going, he will race to beat us to Oneth."

Lutherian grabbed Kim in a bear hug and kissed her. "You are always a wonder to me, sweetling. You are brave and wise beyond your years. Go now and warn the Destroyers." Kim flew to Huw, gave him a big smacking kiss on his lips, and then disappeared.

Huw continued to play his harp with Luther's request over and over again. He smiled with wide-open eyes. Kim's kiss had left him dazed.

"Wipe that silly grin off your face, Huw!" Lutherian roared with laughter and the Crystal and Diamond fairies joined in.

Broadwayne and Cassiarian were walking with Maximillian through the meeting meadow. They spoke to him in a soft voice, answering his many questions. He seemed calmer, and both feys remembered to be cautious with their words.

Cassiarian was just about to ask Maximillian if he wanted to go with them back to the weapons shed when the sound of Huw's harp reached them. Maximillian was startled by the sound and the clear words being sung. He turned to Broadwayne with questioning eyes.

"Well now, I believe we have a little trip to make to the gardens of Coremerick. What say you, Max? Do you want to come with us? We could use your help carrying the barrel of Sasssafras to the fairy sisters.

"What fairy sisters?" Maximillian laughed.

Broadwayne answered his question. "Now, that is going to be a very interesting story to tell you, Max, and we have all the time in the land to start at the beginning."

Both feys decided to bring two barrels of the requested Sassafras filled to the top. They did not wish to make a second trip, considering a storm was brewing in the far distance and their small sailing boat would not fare well if the winds blew their sails off.

Maximillian was sealing the second barrel with wax when Broadwayne announced it was time to go.

"Come on, let us get this Sassafras to the fairy sisters."

Cassiarian flew ahead of the other two feys, and they chased after him. Maximillian could not remember the last time he would have laughed. He enjoyed the feeling and that moment of comfort and safety.

Once the Sassafras was loaded on the boat, they sailed up the coast from Phenloris to Coremerick by way of the Lembath Sea. Hugging the shoreline was the safest way to avoid being caught in the sporadic tidal waves that could potentially throw them farther out to sea. With only three feys aboard, it would be difficult to control the boat.

Broadwayne was at the stern of the small sailing vessel holding on to the rudder as it made its way to Coremerick.

Cassiarian was keeping a watchful eye on Maximillian, who was leaning way too far over the edge as far as he was concerned. "Max, do not fall off this boat. We do not have time to waste fetching you out."

When Maximillian turned to Cassiarian, his smile and wonder were evident. Broadwayne and Cassiarian scrunched their eyebrows and looked at each other. They could not believe Maximillian did not remember the sea.

All three feys were hanging onto a barrel as they floated to the garden and observed the nine fairy sisters sitting in a circle quietly speaking to one another. The last of their supply of Sassafras had done its job, and the garden was once again a lovely wonder to behold.

All heads turned at the sound of Cassiarian's voice.

"As we have been commanded, we bring you not only one but two barrels of the requested Sassafras. The other barrel is still on the ship, and we will fetch it momentarily."

The fairy sisters quickly went to the barrel being lowered to the ground. Red Fairy removed the wax top and nine small fingers came away satisfied it was not at all hot. The cooling winds of the ocean had kept the substance from thickening. This they knew would change its composition, and it would become useless for the desired effect of crystal flower repair and growth.

As if one voice spoke, all nine fairies thanked the feys.

"Where are Luther, Huw, and Glenlillian?" Broadwayne questioned.

It was Brown Fairy who flitted forward and spoke. "They have gone ahead of us to Dolbatheryn."

"Why have they gone to Dolbatheryn, Brown?"

Red Fairy asked them to sit and enjoy a bit of fruit that had just bloomed, and she would explain everything that had happened thus far.

"You say Meirionwen is alive and well, Red?"

"Yes, Cassiarian, and we are in a real pickle here."

Yellow Fairy leaned into Pink Fairy and asked, "What is a pickle?"

"I have no clue," Pink Fairy said.

Then all the fairy sisters laughed at Broadwayne when he asked the same question.

"Never mind," Broadwayne uttered.

It never ceased to startle Merddlyn when Kim disappeared and reappeared before his eyes. Speaking quickly she said, "Everything is settled. My fairies are tending the land at Coremerick and will head to the gardens of Karapalis next. Mother, Grandmother, Huw, and Father are on their way to Dolbatheryn. The plan is for us to get there ahead of Mawrthlyn. Lutherian asks us to lay in wait until they arrive, but if Mawrthlyn discovers us before their arrival, we are to bind him if we can. Meirionwen and Glenlillian have the power to crystal encase him.

"Once that is done, we will be free to make our way to Renewal so we may explain our need to leave the encased Mawrthlyn with her. I understand from our conversations, Merddlyn, that Renewal is fond of Mawrthlyn. I do not think she would be happy seeing our approach with him bound in the crystal before we have a chance to explain ourselves. If we fail to capture and bind him, he will get to the cave at Oneth, and there is no telling what lies will spew from his lips when he gets his audience with Renewal."

Kim moved a strand of hair from her face. After taking a deep breath, she said, "I need to rest a moment and eat something before we continue. My energy is low, and I will be useless in helping you hold onto Mawrthlyn. Please tell me one of you has something that I can eat?"

All three elves came forward with different fruits in their hands, and Merddlyn smiled at their thoughtfulness.

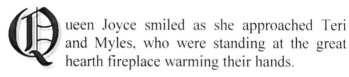

# Chapter Sixteen

Queen Joyce smiled as she approached Teri and Myles, who were standing at the great hearth fireplace warming their hands.

After hugging each of them she asked, "Why have you come back so soon? I thought you planned a few more excursions before heading home. Did you have a pleasant journey? Where are your things?"

"Teri said a great storm was coming, and she wanted us to get ahead of it." Myles gave Teri a little squeeze and smiled.

"We had a wonderful time, Mother. We visited Jahaziel's uncle, Sabastian, before heading home. We graciously accepted his offer to stay the night, and he was very happy to hear how Jahaziel and Siomara are doing. He gave us a few things to take back with us and instructions to give his niece and nephew a letter before the gifts. We brought so many things back with us, we had to purchase a little cart and donkey at a shop and stable near the border before we left. Everything is still in the cart outside, and Mr. Samuel has been kind enough to unharness the donkey. I could not stop myself from laughing when the little donkey started hawing and running after Mr. Samuel. He was trotting toward the stables and did not take his eyes from the dangling carrot Mr. Samuel held in the air."

Princess Teri and Queen Joyce laughed out loud, but their laughter died quickly when Myles did not laugh with them.

With a serious tone to his voice, he said, "Queen Joyce, Teri and I were shocked when we crossed over a newly built walking bridge at the border of North/Southland on our way home. The ocean seems to be seeping up through the land, and I would love an explanation why this is so."

Just then Jahaziel, and Kings William and Crawford, walked over to the couple and told them about the violent shaking of the land around them. Myles wanted to see all the fissures, and as Teri and Joyce excused themselves to help fetch all the gifts, the men walked with Myles and pointed to openings and scattered walking bridges along the way.

"Where is Christopher?" Myles asked.

"He is at the far east end of the border building the last of the bridges. It seems this land has somehow decided to separate itself from North/Southland. We are all relieved that it has not moved much since the first shaking, and I find it quite convenient that I can fish just steps away from home. All I need to bring with me on the short walk is a fishing rod and basket."

Crawford laughed and William and Jahaziel joined in.

Joyce was smiling at Teri's enthusiasm as she unpacked all the gifts and spread them on the floor of the crafting room. Joyce reached for a beautifully made sack that had matching cloth handles and asked Teri what it was.

"Mother, this is a very clever use for old material that would otherwise be discarded. I bought it at a small shop where children's clothes are made." When Teri saw the queen's questioning eyes, she quickly continued, "I went there to purchase new dresses for the fairy sisters and for Kim. I decided on two dresses for Glenlillian, because I could not make up my mind which one to purchase." Reaching into the satchel, Teri carefully removed each dress and set them on the table in front of them.

"Oh, Teri. These are lovely and to think you found them in all these colors."

Maggie came into the room carrying a tray with tea and biscuits, and Agnes and Siomara followed behind her, curious about all the things Teri had lying about. One at a time, Teri gave each of them a gift, and she smiled at their looks of surprise.

After all their hugs and kisses of thanks, Maggie leaned closer and asked, "Did you see all the holes in the ground when you came home, Princess?"

"Yes. How could I not? Was the shaking very bad, Maggie?"

"Well, I will tell you I lost many fine cups and saucers before it finally stopped. I still have the pieces in a bin by the kitchen door that opens to the garden meadow. I do not have the stomach to throw them out just yet."

The women quietly discussed the quaking and formed a plan concerning what they could do to be safe if it happened again.

"Meirionwen, how did you know about Renewal?" Lutherian questioned as they neared Dolbatheryn.

"She was here before we arrived on these shores so many years ago. I do not know of her origins, how she came to find this land, or what her purpose is. If we can manage to straighten this mess out, I will be sure to ask her these questions, Luther."

Glenlillian put a finger to her lips in a gesture for silence. Everyone slowly lowered themselves to the ground, and they were well hidden by the thick forest filled with abundant, beautifully unharmed trees. The meadow they had just crossed was filled with different varieties of fruit bushes. Some of the bushes were a species they had never seen before, and the lovely scent of a thousand different flowers filled the air.

In the softest whisper, Glenlillian warned, "Someone approaches."

Huw was the first to see them, and he raised himself up to the top of a tree. Scouting to be certain the Destroyers of Darkness were not followed, he waited until they reached Glenlillian and the others before he joined them.

A storm was brewing in the distance, and Meirionwen apologized that they could not have a fire. Kim was rubbing her hands together, and Huw came to her and blew his warm breath into them. She smiled and leaned into him, and he put his arms around her and squeezed her tightly. She needed his comfort and the comfort of the others. Kim said a silent prayer for a bit more quiet time before all mayhem broke loose.

When Huw realized Kim had fallen asleep in his arms, his heart skipped a beat, and he fell even more deeply in love with his promised sweet than he had on the day of their ceremony. On occasion he would question himself and wonder about Kim's trust in him. He knew she trusted Jahaziel; but as he held her, he knew she most assuredly did trust him.

Glenlillian smiled at Huw and wondered if her grandfairies could find love like Kim and Huw's and hers and Lutherian's. In the quietness of her mind, she began the list of possible feys that may be ready to promise.

Kim jerked awake. Mirrorme was yelling, *Kim, fly. Fly now*! Kim yelled at the top of her lungs for everyone to fly.

The ball of fire came from the meadow and was heading straight for them. Mawrthlyn knew they were there. The fire hit a tree, and it flamed quickly. The percussive sound threw Lutherian, Huw, and Meirionwen backward, and Kim and Glenlillian had just enough time to grab on to an enormously huge eagle flying away from the shattering noise. Glenlillian asked it to take them to the nearby pond. The eagle dropped them, and they floated to the ground by a bubbling brook that emptied into a river.

They commanded the water to rise as they raised their wings straight up. The pond obeyed, and the water came up and over them. Now, throwing their wings forward, they pointed at the burning tree, and the water quickly doused the hungry flames. The poor tree was moaning, and Glenlillian commanded bees to come to its aid. In a quickly forming swarm, the bees answered, and they slathered the tree down with honey in every spot where they could see charring.

Three bees came to Kim and asked if any fairies were burned. She gently placed them in her hand and rubbed her nose at their little faces.

"Thank you for the offer of your honey, but we are not burned."

The bees quickly left from whence they came, and they were talking to each other in rushed agitated communication with the touching of wings and feet.

Merddlyn and Mawrthlyn flew at each other, and the sound of thunder filled the air as they slammed into one another. Lightning and thunder clapped between them, and they flew from one side of the meadow to the other in swift motion. The fairies and elves jumped into the fray and began winding the vibrating rope around Merddlyn and Mawrthlyn.

"Pull! Everyone pull!" Egwin yelled. The rope tightened, and for just a moment, the wizards passed out. Linden loosened his side of the rope and Farian quickly removed Merddlyn. The others pulled at the rope again, tightening it even more.

Mawrthlyn broke free just as Egwin readied his bow. He aimed, hitting him in his chest dead center. Mawrthlyn screamed, rose up, and spun himself in a vortex of wind. His arms flung out and he threw lightning and thunder everywhere. Then he was gone.

Meirionwen was the first to surface then she slowly climbed out of the pond. The same pond that assisted Kim and Glenlillian just moments ago was uncharacteristically warm. Meirionwen shook herself to clear the fogginess of her mind. She could not recall diving into the pond. Then the others popped up one at a time, gulping in air as they climbed out. They stood close together in shock and were unable to move. The beautiful forest was now a black, charred, smoldering wasteland.

Meirionwen, Glenlillian, and Kim were crying, and there was no consoling them. The tree that was saved moments ago now lay dead in a smoldering heap. No sound emitted from its depths, and Lutherian's heart broke at the sight of it.

"I do not think all the Sassafras in the land can heal this," Huw mumbled.

Mirrorme finished washing the muck off of her cape in the little creek she came upon and was looking for a place to hang it when she heard the explosion. Her cape was discarded, and she ran quickly toward the sound. Halfway to where Mirrorme believed the sound came from, she stumbled upon the black wizard passed out under a rocky overhang. Blood was gushing out of a wound where an arrow was embedded.

She was slap mad angry, but she did not want the wizard to die. When she heard the explosion, she knew the implications of that sound. She was certain he had caused the explosion, and Mirrorme was bound and determined to bring him to justice. Quickly, she gathered up a handful of moss and went back to the black figure. She bent down, yanked the arrow out, and shoved the moss into the hole before Mawrthlyn screamed. When he started to get up, Mirrorme slammed a rock down hard on top of his head, and Mawrthlyn fell unconscious once again. Mirrorme tied Mawrthlyn up with a long rope she kept tied to her waist. Brown Fairy had given it to her to hold her secure when she went rock climbing for bird's eggs.

Mirrorme smiled recalling her words. *"This is made with fairy magic, Meme. It will not break, no matter how rough you treat it."*

Mirrorme had had just about enough of all the nonsense. She dragged Mawrthlyn behind her as she headed in the direction of the explosion, mumbling complaints to herself the entire way. *Pig-headed, foulmouthed wizard. What in tarnation is wrong with you? Do you not have one ounce of sense in that overly large head of yours? Not to mention, you smell to high heaven! Look how much time has been wasted looking for you, you fool.*

Mirrorme stopped and kicked Mawrthlyn hard. When he did not wake, she continued on her journey, dragging the wizard behind her once again.

Everyone was stunned when Mirrorme dumped Mawrthlyn at Merddlyn's feet.

Merddlyn looked at her and winked. "Is this a gift for me, Meme? Really, you should not have." Mirrorme smiled, blushed, and snorted.

Egwin was scratching his head as he looked at Mirrorme. "Are you sure he is not dead, Meme? He looks dead."

Kim, her mother, and grandmother were momentarily shocked by the sudden twist of fate. Once they snapped out of their brain pause, they quickly glided to Mirrorme and began talking to her all at once. Meirionwen ask for silence when she realized Mirrorme could only speak in her mind. "Meme, I am Meirionwen, Diamond Fairy. I am very pleased to meet you."

Mirrorme smiled at the fairy but started backing away from her when Meirionwen attempted to place a hand on her forehead.

"Meme, please be still. I will not hurt you."

Mirrorme opened her eyes wide in surprise, but she held still for the fairy. Meirionwen's hand was warm, and Mirrorme's eyes slowly drifted close. As Meirionwen held her hand in that position for a few quiet moments, all could hear her whispering ancient words in her native tongue. When she finished, she spoke.

"Meme, you now have the gift of speech. You may talk as you wish or not if that is your desire. It is my gift to you for your bravery and help."

Mirrorme opened her mouth and said in a clear voice, "Thank you!"

Then she burst into tears, and Merddlyn went to her. He held her and spoke comforting words. When Mawrthlyn began to stir, Linden hit him with another rock.

"We are not far from Oneth, Merddlyn. I, for one, am anxious to get this over with."

"Meirionwen, can you go ahead and speak to Renewal?" Luther questioned.

"Yes. I will go now."

Maximillian was enjoying all the attention from several of the fairies. Broadwayne and Cassiarian were speaking to Red and Blue Fairy, and White Fairy was trying to figure out how they could carry two barrels full of Sassafras to the gardens and beyond. She knew Brown Fairy was strong and only needed another to help, but she was worrying over safety issues.

Broadwayne walked over to her and said, "Is something wrong with the Sassafras, White?"

"No, Broad. I was just thinking since you are already here we could use your help distributing all this Sassafras. But there is more damage beyond Cormerick's gardens, and we need to fix those areas as well. Then we head on to Karapalis, Llander, and Inisgoud. Since you and Cassiarian are fey guards, you can insure our safety while we travel and pour the Sassafras. I will feel more at ease knowing that we will not have to keep looking behind us at every moment."

"I do not have a problem with that. Let me go ask Max and Cass what they think."

Maximillian and Broadwayne went back to the sailing boat to gather their weapons. If there was trouble ahead, they wanted to be ready to defend the fairy sisters.

Addressing Cassiarian, Broadwayne dropped the weapons on the ground and said, "I thought we brought more weapons with us. Your bow and arrows, my sword and dagger, and one spiked ball and chain are not enough."

Cassiarian laughed out loud. "What sort of trouble were you expecting, Broad? We certainly do have enough weapons. Besides, if we had more who would carry them anyway?"

"I would." Brown Fairy came forward and smiled at Broadwayne. He was considered quite tall for a fey and large of muscle. Brown Fairy was his exact height, and he liked the look of her.

"I imagine you certainly could, Brown." Cassiarian smiled.

"Maybe you can come back with me to the ship, and we can rummage for more weapons," Broadwayne quipped.

Brown Fairy laughed loudly and shook her head. "Are you trying to get me alone with you, Broad?"

"If it were other circumstances, Brown, I certainly would try, but we all need to be careful while we journey to the other clans. We must be on guard at all times."

Brown Fairy nodded her head in agreement, and they made their plans of distribution and travel.

# Chapter Seventeen

Huw and Lutherian made a makeshift travois to haul Mawrthlyn in. Mirrorme and Merddlyn volunteered to pull him along to Oneth, and everyone walked in silence. Mirrorme's face turned red when her stomach growled and everyone realized it had been a while since they had all eaten. Meirionwen and Glenlillian were speaking to each other and Linden, Egwin, Farian, Huw, and Lutherian were in deep conversation of their own. Kim was the only one not engaged in conversation, and she let her mind drift to kings and queens, princes and princesses, and Jahaziel, and then she disappeared.

Shouts were heard far and wide from the group, and Glenlillian shouted the loudest. "Kim, you get back here this instant!" It took Meirionwen a while to calm everyone down before she spoke.

"Kim is with Renewal. She wanted a little time alone with her before our arrival and unloading of Mawrthlyn."

Everyone's why was answered with three words from Meirionwen. "Buy her command."

Kim slowly became aware of her surroundings. She did not recognize where she was, and she was startled when a female voice spoke to her.

"Kim Gold Fairy, I bid you welcome. If you go to the rock table to your left, you will find food and drink. Please help yourself, and I will tell you why I have brought you here." Kim's eyes were wide open, and she did not realize she had spoken out loud.

"Renewal?"

"Yes. I am Renewal. I am pleased to make your acquaintance. Please eat. Your energy is very low and that is not a good position for a fairy to be in."

Kim glided to the table and her stomach growled at the sight of the feast before her. With great enthusiasm, Kim began to stuff her face with the smaller fruits. Finally, she grabbed a kiwi and shoveled it in her mouth and tried to speak at the same time. When she started choking, an invisible hand tapped her back to right her.

"I am so sorry, Renewal. I did not realize I was so hungry."

"Are you feeling better now?"

"Yes, thank you. Oh, is that gukasmasholie in that bowl?" Kim pointed.

Renewal's laughter made Kim smile. "Yes it is. I understand that is a favorite recipe of yours. Please help yourself and tell me if I have come close to yours."

Kim picked up one of many small spoons arranged in a circle around the wooden bowel, placed a little gukasmasholie on a small clay platter, scooped a fair amount into her mouth, and closed her eyes in appreciation.

"I believe your recipe is much better, Renewal. If Red finds this, I can guarantee there will be none left for the others." Kim turned around when Renewal mentioned the cotton cloths at the other end of the table. She nodded and picked one up, and then wiped her face and fingers.

"I believe the others will be arriving here shortly, but I want to speak to you alone. You are going to have a very difficult task to perform for me. This task involves Jahaziel."

Kim's eyes were wide open once again, and she looked around as she spoke. "Do you know Sir Jahaziel?"

"I know every creature and human that occupies this land. I have spent much of my existence watching, Kim."

"Do you wish for Sir Jahaziel to do something for you, fetch something?"

"No, sweetling. I need you to listen to me now. Can you do that without interrupting me?" Kim was embarrassed and she nodded her head but said nothing further. When a door opened at a far wall, Renewal asked Kim to join her in her chamber.

The fairies and feys were moving slower and slower. They were exhausted after tending and repairing Inisgoud's damaged forest and garden. Llanider did not take as much time, but Inisgoud nearly wiped out all of their energy. They were close to Dolbatheryn. Pink Fairy started complaining, and she realized no one was listening to her so she spoke louder.

"Can we please just sit here a moment? My arms are aching and my back is killing me."

The fey guards were used to hard labor and training, but they could see the fairy sisters needed to rest.

"Let me see if I can find us a few things to eat." Cassiarian left with Maximillian and the sack Broadwayne handed him. As the fairies sat in a circle and began to braid each other's hair, Broadwayne smiled in appreciation. It had been a long time since he had seen such a simple fairy task. He smiled again when he heard them whispering words to one another that he could not understand. His own mother and her cousin had died in an accident long ago, and he had no other fairy relatives. When they started singing a song he knew, he got up from his resting place and joined them. His baritone voice was beautiful, and the fairy sisters encouraged him to keep singing with them.

Finally, Maximillian and Cassiarian came back with a few fruits and vegetables, and everyone enjoyed the small feast. Broadwayne lifted Brown Fairy and set her on her feet.

"I know we are tired, but this is the last stop before we reach Oneth. Come on, let us get this over with."

Everyone groaned and complained, but they followed Broadwayne nonetheless.

There were no hoots of laughter or joyful comments as they approached Dolbatheryn. Not one area inside or outside of the gardens was recognizable. Its evident destruction was something they were not prepared for, as a charred wasteland lay before them. Smoldering trees blackened by a powerful force stood in eerie silence. Their branches stripped of leaves looked as if they were reaching out and up for help in a last bid for life. The fairies and feys hugged each other in a tight circle and no consolation could be found.

"There is nothing we can do here that will right this wrong." Cassiarian's despondent voice broke the silence and he continued. "We head to Oneth."

Merddlyn lowered the travois to the ground and checked his vibrating rope and Brown Fairy's rope to be sure Mawrthlyn could not escape when he woke.

"I cannot believe we have finally arrived, Merddlyn," Glenlillian quipped.

"Renewal knows we are here. She bids us to come in to the cave."

Meirionwen nodded to Glenlillian, and they went ahead to ensure the cave entrance was open. Mirrorme bent down, and she and Merddlyn lifted the travois once again and dragged it behind the feys and elves.

When they saw the approach of the fairy sisters along with Maximillian, Broadwayne, and Cassiarian, Mirrorme dropped her end of the travois and ran to the group.

"We finally made it!" Green Fairy hollered.

Huw flitted forward and calmed everyone down. He could clearly see their exhaustion and sorrow and said, "Well done, fairies. I cannot tell you how happy I am to see Max, Cass, and you, Broad. I did worry about their safety, and I see that there was no need. Is everything taken care of, Cass?"

"Almost everything, Huw."

Huw nodded and understood they had seen Dolbatheryn's destroyed gardens.

"Do not worry over it. There are many here who can heal the land. Let us not wake the sleeping wizard with too much discussion before we get him in the cave. Glenlillian and Meirionwen have already gone inside, and we should not be hovering out here having a reunion," Huw said.

Everyone entered the cave single file and in silence. Merddlyn and Mirrorme were the last to enter.

It took them a moment to adjust to the low light, and Mirrorme quickly went to Kim when she heard her crying. Meirionwen was nowhere to be found, and Glenlillian was unsuccessful in calming Kim down.

"Kim, please do not cry. We are all here now," Mirrorme spoke softly.

Huw went to her and took her into his arms, and Kim immediately stopped her tears. His comforting arms were exactly what she needed at that moment. Glenlillian rose and went to Lutherian. Her soft voice informed him that Kim was told something distressing.

"Meirionwen will be back shortly. Renewal summoned her to the other side of the cave. We are to wait here," Glenlillian announced.

Lutherian hugged her and leaned against a wall. When he moved away from it, Glenlillian could not help her laughter. His words echoed around him and everyone stared in awe. "Glen, these walls are breathing."

The fairy sisters could not help themselves. They each went to a wall and gently touched it.

Mirrorme joined them, and she smiled saying, "Do you hear the music?"

They nodded and moved away from the walls, and then they rushed to Mirrorme's side, talking to her and giggling all at once.

"Yes, I can speak. Is it not a wonder? It was Meirionwen who gave me a voice that can be heard, but I still have my inside voice, too." When their eyes focused on the table of food, water, and juices from several fruits in strange-looking cups, they rushed over and began to eat and drink. Mirrorme joined them, and they ate until they could eat no more. Huw, Lutherian, and the rest of the group joined them, and they spoke in quiet conversation.

Merddlyn stayed well away from everyone with his back to the closed cave entrance. His brother was still tied tightly in the travois and unconscious or, he thought, playing dead.

Kim was distressed. Jahaziel could feel it. Christopher's voice was fading in and out, and Jahaziel was overcome with a feeling of foreboding. He stood quickly then looked around and heard the sound of Myles's voice, which seemed far away at first. When Myles touched his shoulder, Jahaziel snapped back from wherever his mind had gone.

Myles repeated his question, but it was clear to William, Crawford, Christopher, and Myles that something was not quite right with Jahaziel.

"What do you think, Jahaziel?"

"What? I am sorry, Myles. Could you repeat your question please?" Jahaziel said.

Myles and Christopher looked at King William with questioning stares.

"Are you all right, Jahaziel? Please is not a word you often use. Would you care to share your thoughts with us?"

"I am sorry, but I need to find Kim. Something is wrong. I do not know what it is, but I feel she needs me."

"Jahaziel, you cannot go to her every time you think something is wrong. She has a family and husband to tend to her. You are needed here at the moment. I am sure if Kim had a need for you, she would send your ring to you, would she not?"

When the eagle's screech echoed in the distance Jahaziel looked at the king and said, "Her message comes now, William."

Meirionwen walked to the assembled and announced, "This is Empress Renewal of the house of Twaitshun, Carouselling, Makluthines, and Strenicious, protector of the lands of Wenlik, Dolan, and Northland, queen of Arrgoniea, and princess of Landslenic."

As Renewal walked from the far left corner of the cave, a resounding gasp was heard. In a singular show of deep respect, everyone present bowed low to the empress.

She was an extremely tall creature, and the top of her head nearly touched the top of the cave's receiving chamber. Her waist-length, reddish-brown hair gently swayed with her graceful movements as she slowly approached them. On her head was a splendid tiara of gold and silver encrusted with diamonds that sparkled in a near-blinding array. The skin of her face and hands was an illuminating shade of white, much like the rare pearls seldom found hiding within the safety of clam muscles, and her features were humanlike. Her dress was a long singular piece of dark cream-colored fabric that fell to the floor and was made of a material not familiar. It had a splendid sheen to it and seemed to float around her with each step she took. The neckline of the dress was gathered and tied together at each end of her shoulders, discreetly revealing her collarbone and long, slender neck. The braided ribbon, in several darker shades of cream and green, cascaded down the dress sleeves to her wrists where they were tied off and playfully dangled to her fingertips.

The golden chain that wrapped around her waist several times was clasped together at their ends with a round diamond-encrusted broach. She was of true regal bearing, and when she spoke, the soft sound of music could be heard.

"Please rise, my friends, and make yourselves comfortable."

Renewal clicked her fingers and stone chairs began to come up from the ground all around them. "If you are still hungry, there is plenty more food and drink at the serving stone. I will be glad to join you since it has been a while since I have eaten."

The group rose and some of them went to the table, while others sat in the offered chairs. Mirrorme was stuffing her face again, and she smiled at Renewal's approach.

"You are, Mirrorme?"

"Yes, ma'am."

"Please, call me Renewal."

"Sure. No problem."

Her smile was bright and Renewal liked the fact that Mirrorme was not overly impressed by her regalness. She smiled back.

"I do not know what these are, but, oh my, they are delicious."

Mirrorme shoved another of the wheat bread honey balls stuffed with vegetables into her mouth and tried to talk at the same time.

"I would love to have this recipe, Renewal."

The empress's laughter bounced all around the cave, and everyone stopped what they were doing and looked at them.

"I will be sure to give it to you before you leave, Meme."

She wandered around quietly speaking with everyone then finally made her way to Merddlyn and Mawrthlyn. When she looked down at the still bound wizard, a look of profound sadness came over her.

Finally, she looked up at Merddlyn and spoke. "I am truly sorry it has come to this, Shoshun, but I cannot allow him anymore time to walk this land with his dark intentions."

Merddlyn smiled at her pet name for him, and he hugged Renewal.

Mirrorme wiped her hands on her dress and walked to the wizard and empress, and then spoke quietly so she would not wake Mawrthlyn.

"I am truly sorry that Mawrthlyn has suffered from this mental difficulty. His insanity has removed much of who he is, and another persona has taken his place. Do you think you can cure him, Renewal?"

Her comment stunned them, and in a rush of words they asked, "What is this you speak of, Meme? We do not understand your words. Please explain this."

Complete silence filled the room, and everyone turned to Mirrorme. She was a little startled but kept her composure.

"I was told this story before I swam to this land with my great aunt." She closed her eyes, took a deep breath, and began her story.

"When at sea in its deepest regions, a few maids stayed longer than allotted, and they ignored the time calendar. They swam to unheard of depths searching for the mythical land of Loveliness. It is an ancient story handed down from generation to generation that tells of a blue stone that rests inside a giant clamshell in a land no longer occupied. This stone has the power to bestow eternal life to the mermaid who finds it. At that depth, the sea causes great suffering within the mind of the mermaid searching for the blue stone and other known treasures and confusion enters the mind. Their exhaustion was forgotten and they continued with their search. Consumed by the idea of immortality, they did not think to eat or rest. Once the depth illness begins, in most cases it cannot be stopped. As it slowly entered their minds, they went insane, swimming even deeper into the ocean depths, thinking they were going up instead of down. They continued swimming with hopes of breaking the surface, but the darkness enveloped them and they eventually mind separated or, in some cases, died. Some mermaids have been found floating in the surf, but they were no longer themselves."

Meirionwen floated over to them and asked the question on everyone's mind. "Can this mental difficulty be cured Meme?"

"Yes, with time, care, and ancient medicines it was sometimes possible. However, not everyone could be helped. Eventually the affected mermaid would succumb and pass from life. I know nothing of these ancient people and even less of the therapies used, but I can try to seek them out for you, Renewal."

Merddlyn's spirits lifted, and he was grateful that Renewal was willing to wait for answers before her final decision to place Mawrthlyn in endless suspension.

"Meirionwen and Glenlillian, would you please come forward. We shall crystal encase Mawrthlyn to preserve him until Meme returns with her information," Renewal said.

Renewal bent down to Mawrthlyn. She placed her hand on his forehead then said softly, "Sleep deeply, my little wizard. Sleep."

Merddlyn hugged Mirrorme and kissed her on her lips. She was stunned by that, but even more stunned by his words. "You may have saved the life of my brother, Meme, and you may have saved his mind as well. I did not know it was lost. I did not know his constant angers would do this to him. I have hope now; hope that I did not have before. To believe he may be repaired, returned to his own mind to be released from this darkness that has claimed him is unbelievable to me. You are such a wonder, Meme, and my heart is now yours for the asking."

Mirrorme was overwhelmed that her hopes and dreams of being loved came in the form of a handsome, tall wizard.

# Chapter Eighteen

Jahaziel patted the eagle on her head, placed her on his right shoulder, and put his ring on the little finger of his left hand. Knowing the bird could not answer him, Jahaziel questioned her anyway.

"Do you know where she is? Do you know what I am to do at this moment? Should I leave for..."

He did not know where Kim was. He would end up riding in circles trying to decide which way to go. Instead of leaving him, the eagle stayed with Jahaziel, and he was surprised she did not fly away at William's approach and words.

"Well, from this moment I shall be very careful what I say to you, Jahaziel. Your instincts have always been reliable. I think we should all search for Kim. Throw the bird in the air, and we will follow her."

"Christopher, Myles, and I agree. We will go with you and help you search for her. I will collect some provisions and tell Teri and Joyce what we are doing." King Crawford stated.

"I need to let Sara know as well," Christopher said. "Do you think we need weapons, Jahaziel?"

King William pointed ahead of him and let a breath out.

"I think our ride is here, Jahaziel."

Jahaziel turned around and beheld the two unicorns approaching them. William's smile was brilliant, and he spoke to the pair. "I do believe you have come to assist us in some way. Am I correct, Elaine, Enos?" When they spoke, Jahaziel was startled.

"Sir Jahaziel. We have been summoned to come here and take you to Kim. King William may accompany you. We will leave when the sun sets. It is much safer for us to travel at night," Elaine said.

"William, do you suppose you could tell Sir Jahaziel about our unique means of travel?" Enos asked. They thought King William had lost his mind. He laughed so hard he fell to the ground, and the unicorns joined him in his laughter.

Kim was flitting back and forth in an agitated state. When Huw tried to calm her down, she flew out of the cave and threw up in a bush. It was when Huw placed a hand on her forehead to comfort her that he discovered her burning fever. Immediately, he flew to Glenlillian and told her that Kim was ill.

Renewal was at Kim's side before the others arrived. With gentle movement, she carried the fairy back into the cave and around to a restricted area. She closed the rock door behind her and gently placed Kim on a soft bed.

"You have made yourself sick with sorrow, Kim. Sweetling, you cannot let Sir Jahaziel see you in this state. He will not do as I ask if he sees you are beside yourself with grief. You must be strong so he will be strong. He will feel that and be more settled in his mind. It will help him understand my decision and not fight me on it. Can you sit up?"

Kim nodded and took the cup offered her. As she sipped the healing tea, she let Renewal's words sink in. Kim knew Renewal was right. Jahaziel had bonded with Kim upon their first meeting, and he would feel her distress. She knew he would kill himself to get to her if need be.

Kim drank the last of the tea then rose up to meet Renewal's eyes. She smiled and kissed Renewal on the cheek.

"I must apologize to you, Renewal. I have only been thinking of myself, and I let my sorrow overwhelm me. Jahaziel deserves more from me, and I will show him my strength, thereby strengthening him in return. May I stay here a moment longer to collect myself before I return to the others?"

"Yes. Of course. You may stay as long as you like. Elaine and Enos are at this very moment arriving at Fitzhuwlyn to collect Sir Jahaziel and King William. They will wait for the setting of the sun before taking flight. I have asked Enos to bring the king for moral support. You have time to take a well-needed nap, Kim."

"Thank you, Renewal. Would you please tell my mother and Huw that I am feeling better and not disturb me while I nap?" Renewal nodded and left the tiny room. Before she closed the rock door, she heard Kim's words and her laughter. "I do not think they will have an easy time convincing Jahaziel to ride on a horse that can fly."

Glenlillian and Meirionwen rushed to Renewal and she smiled. "Kim is well and taking a nap at the moment. She has come to her senses and sees her behavior is harming Jahaziel, not helping him. She is a very brave fairy, Glenlillian. You should be most proud."

When Renewal said nothing further, the fairies looked at each other and wondered what Jahaziel had to do with any of it.

Jahaziel's stomach stopped growling, and his heart stopped pounding. His mind told him Kim was calmer somehow, and he closed his eyes, took in a deep breath, and let it out slowly. He did not know how it was possible when moments ago she was so emotional, but he was thankful for it. Hysterical women were one thing, but a hysterical fairy could be dangerous.

King William approached Jahaziel with the saddled unicorns. "I have put these specially made saddles on Elaine and Enos, Jahaziel. It will allow their wings freedom and make us more comfortable and secure on the ride to Oneth." The king burst into laughter once again and said, "Just do not look down, Jahaziel. I fear you would fall out of your saddle!"

Jahaziel stared in wonder at the sight before him. Elaine and Enos stood nineteen hands tall. The strong flexible rotational quadrant of the unicorn's wings were located at the shoulder and followed down to the arm. It was the most muscular part at its thickest point where the feathers layered themselves in a tight and narrow cascade. From there the larger feathers could expand and contract, much like the feathers of large birds spanning back to their hearth, girth, barrels, and flanks. As the feathers continued to follow the contour and curve of their back couplings, they reached their long tapering ends at the hips, stifles, and gaskins.

The unique saddles were barely visible under all the feathers, and Jahaziel shook his head, thinking it was a dream he could not wake from.

"Is it necessary to frighten the knight, King William?" Elaine spoke with concern.

"Do not concern yourself with Jahaziel's feelings, Elaine. Not much frightens Crawford's knight. I was just teasing him to lighten his mood."

"Oh, I understand. To lighten one's mood is a good thing, a human thing." Enos nodded in agreement then Elaine spoke once again.

"When you are ready, Sir Jahaziel, I will not move while you gain your saddle. You may hang on to my withers and your leg straps will hold you tightly around my girth. We will then begin by walking at a normal gate. Once you have a feel for us, we will increase our pace to a trot and then we will rise. It will be a smooth transition, I assure you. However, if you feel the need to look down, may I suggest that you do not do so. We will be flying at a swift pace. As you hold tightly with your legs, lean in to our necks. Otherwise, the wind may knock you clean out of your saddles."

"That was a good one, Elaine. If you lighten their moods anymore, they can float to Oneth," Enos stated.

When the unicorns started laughing out loud, William and Jahaziel looked to the heavens for patience.

William spoke, and Jahaziel agreed. "You see, Jahaziel. They are just like children. One needs to be very careful what one says in front of them."

The knight and king mounted the unicorns, and Myles tightened King William's leg straps while Christopher tightened Jahaziel's. Satisfied that they were both secure, the men stepped away.

King Crawford nodded and said, "Ready Jahaziel?"

"No, Crawford, but I believe that no longer matters."

The unicorns thanked Myles and Christopher, nodded to King Crawford, and then began a slow gate followed by a trot, and moments later they gave warning as they lifted themselves into the air. William and Jahaziel leaned into the unicorns as instructed, and they slowly disappeared from sight.

"We have seen many strange things these past few years, Christopher, King Crawford, but never in my wildest imagination would I have thought horses could fly. Pigs maybe? But not horses." Christopher and Crawford burst out laughing as they followed Myles into Fitzhuwlyn Castle. Christopher needed to collect a few of his belongings and his horse before heading back to Allenwood. The crescent moon made for easy travel, and they talked of other things as they entered the heart room.

"Are you sure you do not want to go back with me to Allenwood, Myles? I convinced Sara to try her hand at cooking, and from what I hear from your head cook Winifred, Sara is an artist. Apparently her food looks as good as it tastes."

"Teri and I will be along tomorrow. She wants to spend the night visiting her parents a bit longer. Lots of talk of where we went and all the things we saw, ate, and drank on our after-wedding trip, no doubt. If you need anything from our craftsmen hut, just leave a list with Robert. I will bring it with us in the morning. Would you like some wine or mead before you leave?"

"Yes, thank you. It should keep me warm on the ride home." Myles smiled at Christopher's reference that Allenwood was now his home.

Everyone was waiting for Jahaziel and King William. The fairy sisters were gathered around several rock chairs, and Glenlillian, Meirionwen, and Kim were nibbling a few tasty morsels from the serving stone's long table. Merddlyn was still in conversation with Mirrorme, and Huw and Lutherian were sitting near a fireplace Renewal had lit to warm the open room. Cassiarian and Broadwayne joined Huw, Luther, Egwin, Linden, and Farian at the fire, and they rubbed their hands together over it, enjoying its warmth. Finally, they sat and spoke in quiet tones discussing fey guard concerns. Maximillian was having a private conversation with Renewal, and he was smiling and nodding in agreement at something she had said.

"Would you like me to go with you to the water's edge, Meme?" Merddlyn asked.

"Yes, I would like that. I do not know if I still have the ability to call out to my water ancestors. I have not laid my eyes on many since I was born. Before coming to this land when I was a child, I was told water maids no longer lived in the oceans and that I should adapt to the land and not complain. I have been alone these many years and never questioned that I may be the last of my kind. Long ago I heard a conversation between two others about maids being spotted beyond the Lembath Sea. If they indeed do still exist, I will be surprised if they answer my call. I have never traveled this far north before. I found no reason to do so until now."

"Come then. Let us call to your ancestors."

Merddlyn and Mirrorme walked out of the cave and headed to where the Oneth River met the sea. With his hand in hers, they closed their eyes and sang the song of mermaids.

King William and Jahaziel untied their leg straps, jumped from their saddles, and bent over. They placed their hands on their knees and took deep, cleansing breaths in and out. Both men were light-headed and needed a moment to gain their bearings.

"I am sorry about the sudden turn to the east, King William, but a crosswind was ahead, and we needed to avoid it," Enos stated as if it were an everyday normal occurrence.

The knight and king stood and took their time removing the saddles from the unicorns. Then they thanked them and went in search of the cave opening.

They approached the cave from the west. Its visible face was made of hard granite and stood high above the ground nearly reaching several treetops on each side. The trees had an eerie appearance and seemed to watch the men as they came closer. Like silent sentinels, they stood guard. King William thought the trees were quite creepy looking, and he decided not to touch them. From its highest point down to the sandy ground, the granite wall had a large flat surface. Its gradual wide slope ended at level ground and grass and flowers grew in an abundant array up to the cliff's edge. Had Jahaziel and William walked up the slope to its highest point, they would see the sharp drop to the rock and sandy shore. No one would be the wiser that a cave was inside the mound. Not from a westerly approach, nor from a boat near the shoreline could its entrance be visible. As knight and king stood in silence facing the granite wall, they searched for an opening. King William walked closer and ran his hand gently over the surface. Suddenly, a swishing noise was heard, and the opening appeared before them.

With a bit of trepidation, Jahaziel and King William walked in with slow, cautious steps. Once they passed an overhang, they turned to their right and headed toward the sound of voices, light, and warmth.

The king and knight stood at the entrance to Renewal's receiving chamber and stared in wonder. The chamber was huge and looked like any normal room with chairs, tables, and a fireplace. It took a moment for them to realize everyone had stopped talking and all eyes were turned to the men standing in the entryway.

Kim hollered his name and quickly flew to Jahaziel. Renewal did not miss the knight's huge smile or Kim's delight in seeing him.

"Did you have a good flight, Jahaziel?"

Kim could not help herself and laughed until tears came to her eyes. Then the entire room broke into laughter, and Kim rose up and began to play with Jahaziel's hair, trying to flatten it with swift movements.

"Stop that! Leave me alone, you daft fairy!" he roared, and then he slapped at his hair and at Kim.

Renewal's hand went over her mouth in an effort to hide her laughter.

"You look like you have been struck by lightning, Jahaziel. Your hair and William's is standing up in several places and the rest is, is…"

Laughter again broke out, and Jahaziel grabbed Kim, gave her a swift hug, and then set her away from him as he spoke with sincere words.

"Are you all right? I got here as soon as I was able."

He released her, took off his ring, and handed it back to her saying, "Your eagle has once again returned my ring to me, Kim." He finished with a smile. She quickly held it to her chest for a moment then put it back where it belonged on her wrist.

Renewal finally understood just how strong their bond truly was, and the love they had for one another was evident even to the smallest of creatures.

Her heart grew heavy knowing she had to break that bond if they were to survive the separation. When tears formed in her eyes and slowly began to fall down her cheeks, she was taken aback by them. She had never cried before.

"Jahaziel!" Huw hollered. When the fey approached the knight, his smile was genuine. "Come and have a bit of food and wine. You see William is already helping himself and may only leave you a morsel if you do not push him aside." Jahaziel smiled and patted the fey on the shoulder and said, "It is good to see you, Huw. Has Kim been giving you fits?"

Huw nodded at their shared experience of Kim's near hysteria, and they were both glad it was over.

Jahaziel followed Huw to the long table and started to eat a few small pieces of fruit. When William bellowed, Jahaziel turned to him with questioning eyes.

"Jahaziel! You have to try these. They are called stuffed mushrooms, and they are delicious." He handed one to Jahaziel, and he could not help smiling at William's nod and wide-open eyes. Then someone handed him a cup of wine, and he turned to thank the person.

His smile was frozen upon his face. King William's eyes were wide and they looked at the tall creature smiling at them in wonder.

196

Renewal nodded her head and spoke.

"I am very pleased to meet you, Sir Jahaziel, King William. Thank you for answering my call so quickly. When you are finished enjoying the fare, I would like very much to speak with both of you privately."

All they could do was nod and stare after her as she walked to Meirionwen and Glenlillian.

Kim was speaking with Huw, and she knew what he wanted to ask her, so she spoke quickly. "I am fine, really, Huw. Do not worry. I will not make a scene."

"I did not think you would. You know I am very fond of Jahaziel, and I understand his concern for you. I am here for you, and you can come to me without fretting about my feelings. I am not jealous of Jahaziel, and I am thankful for his friendship to both of us."

Kim hugged him and stayed at his side, nervously waiting for the storm that would surely come.

King William introduced Jahaziel to Egwin and Linden. In turn the elves introduced the men to Farian, and they struck up a conversation. Jahaziel tried to concentrate on their words, but his mind kept wandering back to the face of the tall female creature.

*What possible reasons did she have for summoning us to this meeting,* Jahaziel pondered.

# Chapter Nineteen

Elaine and Enos were nibbling on sweet grass when Merddlyn and Mirrorme approached them. Mirrorme's eyes were wide with wonder, and Merddlyn smiled at the pair.

"How good it is to finally meet you, Merddlyn. It has been a long time since we were told the story about a powerful sleeping wizard by our forest friends at Newry and we are glad to see you have awakened," Enos said. Elaine nodded and kept chewing on her grass. "I am Enos and this is Elaine."

"Yes, it is good to meet you both as well. Let us not let too much time pass before our next visit." Turning to Mirrorme, Merddlyn introduced her to the pair. "This is my very good friend, Mirrorme. Meme, this is Elaine and Enos." She smiled a bright smile and began to stroke the unicorn's manes as she stood between them.

"I am very pleased to meet you. You do not appear to be human. Are you elven?"

"Mirrorme is a land mermaid, Elaine," Merddlyn answered.

"How wonderful. Do you see any of your family or water ancestors, Mirrorme?"

"No, Elaine. I appear to be the only one of my kind here. When I was very young I was told by a very old maid that my people no longer lived in the seas. I never did get a complete explanation, and I did not question the elderly maid. Please call me Meme."

"Will you be heading back to Newry?" Merddlyn asked.

"Yes. After we drop off Sir Jahaziel and King William at Fitzhuwlyn Castle we will head home. Our business with the prince and princess is at an end; we are ready to walk among our lands once again. Hopefully before the sun rises and cooks us all. These temperatures have changed so quickly that I have not had a chance to enjoy the cooler weather before the heat decided to descend upon us yet again." Enos said.

"I believe you wish to try and contact your family, your people, if it indeed it is possible, Meme. Have you had any luck?" Elaine questioned.

Mirrorme was stunned by her words.

"How do you know that I am seeking them?"

"We heard your beautiful song, and we understand its meaning. If you like, we can fly over the ocean and search. They may be on their way to you."

Mirrorme stared at Merddlyn, who was as shocked by Elaine's words as she was.

"I do not know what to say except thank you. Yes." After nodding to each other, the unicorns took to flight and disappeared from their sight.

Renewal quietly shut the door behind her, William, and Jahaziel. After offering them a seat, she sat in a high-back chair across from them. She took a deep breath, closed her eyes, and quickly said a prayer for patience. She knew her words, no matter how carefully she said them, would no doubt anger the humans.

"My name is Renewal. I am empress to several lands and charged as protector to several more. I have summoned you here to explain the shaking of the ground at the border of this land. Please let me explain everything before you ask your questions."

She waited until they each gave a nod and then she continued.

"It has come to my attention that more and more humans are becoming aware of the existence of fairies, feys, and elves. The possibility of finding creatures not yet discovered greatly increases each day. It is not a position I wish them to be in and, therefore, I have decided to separate this land you call Northland from the land of North/Southland. I am sure you have felt the shaking recently."

Jahaziel leaned in toward Renewal and with squinted eyes he nodded and let her continue.

"All who live here who are not human are my responsibility. I will not allow them to be abused in any way by humans who possess desires of wealth, power, or position. This separation will take place now and will continue on a slow easy path in order to ensure the least amount of damage to both lands. It will be your responsibility, King William and Sir Jahaziel, to assist every human in vacating this land. It is entirely up to you to make it an easy or difficult transition, but leave you must. Those feys and fairies you are already acquainted with will assist you in any way they can, but they are not to show themselves to people they do not know."

Renewal took a moment to breath then continued.

"Kim was not aware of the wheels she set into motion when she decided to take matters into her own hands and heal you, Sir Jahaziel. She ignored the strict rules feys and fairies abide by and broke an important law."

Jahaziel was becoming angry at the suggestion that everything that had happened was Kim's fault, and King William placed a hand on his shoulder to keep him from jumping up and leaving.

Renewal took another breath, "Regardless of Kim's interference, fairies and feys would eventually be discovered over time. Human migration to this land is something I tried to avoid by creating impossible weather with high winds, rain, storms, and, on occasion, snow. It did not detour you or the others from eventually making your homes here in our lands. Therefore, I commanded the seasons to be less harsh and hoped those humans living here would be the last."

Renewal leaned back into her chair and finished her speech. "This land will slowly move away until it can no longer be seen from your shores, and from there it will drift until it is impossible to get to by ship."

Jahaziel jumped up and yelled at Renewal. "You cannot do this! I will not allow it, Renewal. You have no command over me or any other people here. You have no right to take such matters into your own hands and make decisions that carry such dire consequences, such finalities."

Jahaziel's shouting could be heard out in the great hall, and many rushed to the doors to stop Jahaziel before Renewal killed him. Maximillian, Broadwayne, Cassiarian, Luther, and Huw positioned themselves at the door and hovered with their arms crossed in fey guard stance. They would protect Renewal's private audience.

"Jahaziel," King William spoke in a stern voice and stood next to Crawford's best knight. "You cannot yell at this creature. She can end you in a moment. I believe she can do this with a simple stroke of her hand. Watch your words here, my man."

"King William, I need to be alone with Sir Jahaziel. Could you please leave?" Renewal said.

He nodded to Renewal and swiftly left the room. When the others saw King William leaving, they rushed to him. He put up a hand, said nothing, and continued out the main receiving hall and out-of-doors. *I need air*, he told himself, *lots and lots of air*. The shock of Renewal's words was choking him, and he needed to get away from that place.

"Please sit down, Sir Jahaziel," Renewal said in a commanding yet soft voice.

"I do not do any of this lightly. I do this to protect all the creatures of this land from unscrupulous humans. How would you feel if Kim or Luther or Glenlillian were captured and tortured into giving up their magical gifts? Would you not give your life to save hers, Jahaziel? Would you not do the same for her family?"

Jahaziel ran his hands through his hair in frustration. He knew her words spoke the truth. But his heart pounded, and his mind could not think of such a separation.

"What of Kim and myself? Are we to be separated from each other forever, Renewal?"

She took a moment to gather her next words.

"Jahaziel, you must agree to this separation. You know it is for everyone's own good. We, they, will not survive in captivity." Jahaziel looked up at Renewal, and her words suddenly reached his heart and awareness came to him that surprised Renewal.

"You have seen the future, Renewal, a horrible destructive future and are trying to stop it. Is this the only way? Can you not think of another plan?"

"I do not know how you have come to that understanding, Sir Jahaziel, but you are correct. Please do not tell what you have just said to me to anyone in this land. If they knew of this other future, this other reality, all feys and fairies would rather go with the elves to the place where their ancestors of the past reside than be captured. If they do that, I will not be able to follow them there."

"I will not speak of this to anyone," Jahaziel promised. Then he asked, "How much time do we have until the next shaking?"

"You have what you call one week to tell your people that this land will continue to shake until it falls apart into uninhabitable sections. That, of course, is not true, as this land will stay intact; but it should help you convince everyone that they have no choice but to leave the area. This should give you enough time before the next quaking. Then you must begin your exodus in the weeks to come."

When Jahaziel stood, he swayed slightly, and Renewal reached out a hand to steady him.

"I must tell you one more thing before you leave, Jahaziel."

He looked at her with such sad eyes, Renewal could no longer look at him.

"I must remove your bonding with Kim."

For a moment he could not move. When he spoke it was a near whisper. "You stab me in the heart, Renewal, and you expect me to let you?" Jahaziel stormed out and did not stop until he spotted King William standing by the unicorns. He had resaddled them and was patiently waiting for Jahaziel.

Neither the knight nor king said a word as they swung onto the backs of the unicorns, tightened their legs straps, and headed for Fitzhuwlyn.

Huw held Kim tightly to him as they watched Jahaziel storm away, and she looked at her promised one and his heart weighed heavy in his chest from her words.

"Jahaziel is in pain. He gulps in air and presses a fist to his chest. He is trying not to cry, Huw. He is in pain! What did Renewal say to him? He is thinking he is going to die from a broken heart."

Kim could say no more, and she hid her face in Huw's embrace.

Not one of the assembled had a dry eye, as they were all given the understanding of the land separation by Renewal and collectively lowered their heads in prayer. They prayed for Sir Jahaziel and the people who would lose the only homes they knew. They prayed for a smooth transition and separation from North/Southland, and they prayed for themselves.

When Renewal came out of her private room, Mirrorme went to her and placed a crystal vile into her hands then closed her fingers over it.

"My family came through, Renewal. You are to give Mawrthlyn the healing tea with one drop of this elixir added. They said it must be done by your hand alone. He is to have this tea twice, once at sunrise and once at sunset. In five

204

sunrises, he should be showing signs of improvement. If not, there is nothing else that can be done for him."

"Thank you, Meme." Renewal turned to Merddlyn. "Regardless of his condition, it does not release him from judgment. Mawrthlyn has caused much damage and has taken the life of a well-loved elf elder called Darrius. He must be punished for this crime."

Renewal nodded, thanked Mirrorme again, and slowly walked back to her private room and shut the door.

Meirionwen knocked on the door and entered at Renewal's command. She sat down next to the empress and spoke in a soft voice. "Renewal, if you remove Kim and Jahaziel's bonding he will eventually die. Kim is bonded to others, and she is use to it. This is Jahaziel's first and only bonding, and he is a human, not a fey. They have been too connected to one another for far too long. Kim will eventually recover, but I fear Sir Jahaziel will not. He will not recover from their separation as the lands will. In all my life, I have never seen such a thing, such a strong bonding as this. Please do not do this."

With sad eyes, Renewal nodded her agreement, and she disappeared from Meirionwen's sight. She needed to be alone to think upon the journey ahead.

Finally, the assembled eventually left Renewal's cave dwelling. Reappearing, Renewal stopped Merddlyn and Mirrorme at the entrance and smiled. "I will take care of Mawrthlyn and I will be sure he gets the elixir on time. Also I will contact you if I have a need. I will let you know what I have decided concerning his fate once I have had more thought on the matter."

Merddlyn nodded and walked out with Mirrorme by his side.

Renewal rotated her head forward, first to each side then she rolled it to the back of her neck trying to get the kinks out. She walked to a far wall, leaned against it, and spoke.

"I did not think this would be so difficult, Aaron. Why did you not warn me of these humans' attachments to the feys and fairies? King William has become a great friend to an elf called Alywn. He is the son of Darrius. The one whose life Mawrthlyn took. Is this just a coincident do you think?"

The wall breathed in and out and Renewal moved forward and back with each deep breath Aaron took. It was her comfort now, her solace for the time being.

"You know this needed to be done, Renewal. The sooner the better for everyone involved. As far as King William and Alwyn are concerned, it is what it is—a friendship and nothing more. Let the time everyone has be useful in settling down their emotions. In other words, let sleeping dogs lie, Renewal. Go to your room and rest. I will stand watch."

She pushed herself away from the wall and stopped a moment, and then spoke. "Is it not strange, Aaron, that Mawrthlyn and I both seek to rid this land of human habitation?"

"Your way is better. Do not think on the matter any longer. Go."

Renewal entered her sleeping chamber, fell upon her bed, and slept like the dead.

There were so many things that still needed to be done. Glenlillian and Meirionwen went to every fairy clan personally to tell them about the land separation. Trees near the border needed moving. The homes that could not be moved needed to be packed up and taken to new areas. Fairy babies needed to be watched at all times and guinea cavas needed relocating. Finally, when the work of moving everything and everyone to safe distances away from the border began, they were able to spend a little time at their own home to repair willow baskets and pack down anything that could fall and break with the next quaking.

Kim and Huw entered the herb drying room and spoke to them.

"Huw and I thought we would go visit the Concordia Gardens at each clan to be sure they understand the shaking. If they become anxious, we will be sure to pour a little Sassafras on them. If you think they will need anything else, pack it in our grass-woven sacks." Kim smiled at her mother and grandmother and they nodded their agreement.

"We would love to go with you, but we are exhausted from our recent trips to all the clans, and we need a little rest. Did you tell Luther what you are doing? Maybe he would like to go along. He has been very grumpy lately, because he cannot go on an expedition." Glenlillian laughed and winked at Huw.

"I understand from Egwin that you found the time in your busy schedule to visit his father, Richmond, Grandmother," Kim stated.

"Yes. I had the most wonderful reunion with him. We were friends for many years before my accident, and he often accompanied me to my favorite gardens, while I procured herbs and new flowers. When I questioned him about our trips to the gardens, he actually blushed and made me make a fairy promise to tell no one about his love of flowers. It broke my heart to know he had not gone to one garden since his blinding

207

accident. When I returned his sight to him, he actually hollered at me about how unfair it all was. I did not understand at first, then..." Meirionwen's mind drifted back to their conversation.

*"Keep your eyes closed until I tell you to open them Richmond. This sap is cool to the touch and will work quickly." Richmond nodded his head for Meirionwen to begin. Moments later she handed him a soft cloth to wipe off the excess sap and said, "You may open your eyes now, Richmond." His bellowed response was not what she'd expected, and Meirionwen laughed until her sides ached.*

*"Look at you! You have not aged since the day we first met in the meeting meadow at Karapalis. It is not fair, Meiri. Do not dare leave until you have given me back my youthful appearance."*

"I cannot remember the last time I laughed like that."

Meirionwen and Glenlillian waved to Kim and Huw, and they went back to their task of repairing the willow baskets needed for collecting the large amount of herbs recently dried. All of Kim's fairies promised to distribute the healing herbs to the clans that were running low.

The people of Northland were packing all their belongings, much like the fairies, as quickly as they were able. Everyone was waiting for word from King Crawford and King William about securing property at North/Southland and beyond. They knew they could not walk or ride with their wagons in tow into North/Southland with no place to go, no home to settle into. Some people had relatives willing to take them in for a short while, but they were never offered a permanent stay.

The recent meeting Queen Joyce had with the servants, workmen, and gardeners at Fitzhuwlyn helped settle the minds of many, but she spent hours trying to explain what was about to happen concerning their land.

"I am thankful for your patience, and I hope I have answered all of your questions reasonably, but we must do as King William and King Crawford say. I know this will be a difficult move, but we will not be safe here once the land begins to break off into undeterminable pieces. Both kings and Sir Jahaziel have assured me that we will be able to stay and live close together. The king and I consider all of you family, and we would not hear of you going off on your own to seek land and positions unfamiliar to you."

As the meeting came to an end, Queen Joyce was able to take a cleansing breath and truly relax for the first time since the meeting began. She did not like lying to people who had welcomed her with open arms when she first arrived at Fitzhuwlyn so many years ago, but her hands were tied. She would protect those wonderful fairies with her last breath if need be.

Renewal was standing very still. With closed eyes and with an appreciative smile on her face, she listened to the sounds of the ocean. She was patiently waiting just inside her cave opening for the fairies. When she heard the approach of Meirionwen and Glenlillian, she smiled. After they embraced and exchanged pleasantries, Meirionwen spoke. "We are both humbled that you have summoned us to watch the approach of the Crystal Butterflies, Renewal. I always wondered what happened to them after they reached Oneth. We also wish to thank you for the repair of the gardens and forest at Dolbatheryn. None of us had one ounce of strength left to repair such damage."

"You are both most welcome, and I am very happy that you were able to come to witness this exciting event.

"This is their last resting stop before they go on from here. I found them upon my arrival in this land hanging from the Azalea bushes safely enclosed in their cocoons. This place was not yet occupied by elves, fairies, or humans, and I was free to roam around without fear of being seen. I decided to seek a place of refuge for them, and I wandered about an entire full moon before I came upon the cave at Bardfey Island. I took my time crafting a singularly unique crystal chest to place them in for their safety, because I knew these lands would soon be occupied. I did not want them to be discovered until I was sure all their wishes would be granted.

"They sang of their origins in their sleep, and I wrote everything down in several scrolls. I also understood the dire consequences that would fall upon this land if the instructions were not followed exactly. What I did not expect was how long it would take before they were finally discovered by you, Meirionwen. Now, I will tell you their story as it was told to me.

"The Crystal Butterflies came from a faraway land that had suffered a devastating disaster. A long dormant volcano erupted and spewed its flames and lava down to the valley below. These butterflies were the only survivors, and they barely had enough time to gather their cocoon homes and flower seeds before taking flight in search of land capable of growing their crystal flowers.

"Although their energy was running low, it was their hunger that forced them to stop here in these lands. The Azalea bushes were strong enough for them to hang their homes, and so they crawled into their safe havens and went into hibernation.

"These cocoons emitted a sound of distress. Few creatures are capable of hearing such a sound. I am one of those creatures and I came to their aid. As time passed, I understood their own lands would eventually heal and they would seek to return in order to breed and renew their numbers. However, upon their first return after being renewed by this land, the soil in their land was barely capable of growing enough crystal flowers to feed newly hatched butterflies. In order to survive, they decided not to breed. They ate their fill and went into hibernation once again. When they awoke, they headed back to these lands once again to feed and rest."

Renewal smiled once again and invited them into her cave. The fairies sat and listened to Renewal tell them a humorous story about a strange creature from the land of Wenlik that was obsessed with the color blue and how she took great pains to be certain she never wore the color in his presence. When the sound of harp music, clicking, and chirping was heard quickly approaching, Renewal nodded at the fairies.

"Shhh, be very still and enjoy the experience."

Meirionwen and Glenlillian smiled at Renewal. In swift motion, the butterflies entered in one long rush.

Once inside, they quickly searched for places to light upon. Flicking and clicking their wings, they finally settled upon the walls of the cave. Aaron hummed to them, and they clung to the living wall. Settled and happy, they fell into a deep sleep. The cave walls sparkled in the low light as the butterflies were gently rocked back and forth with the slight movements of Aaron's breathing.

"Will they stay here, Renewal, as our land floats away?" Glenlillian whispered.

"Yes, Glenlillian. When they awaken, they will go ahead of us, leading the way to their land of origin. This is the reason the butterflies have returned. Their destinies and ours are now tied together. This was our purpose, our fate, to join this land with their land. This land now follows the flight of the Crystal Butterflies.

Siomara walked quickly into the kitchen to speak to the queen, who was in deep conversation with Maggie.

"I think that should do it, Your Majesty," Maggie smiled.

"Yes, I agree. Let us put them into the small fireplace in the great hall. They should bake quickly and more evenly, do you not think?"

Queen Joyce turned at the sound of Siomara clearing her throat. "What is it, Siomara?"

"You have visitors, Your Majesty. I went ahead and showed them to the sewing room."

"Thank you." Turning to Maggie the queen said, "Would you mind putting this bread in to bake on your own? You are an exceptional cook and baker, Maggie, and I trust you will know exactly when all the banana bread is finished."

Maggie smiled at the compliment and nodded.

The queen and Siomara walked to the sewing room and stood in the doorway with eyes open wide and huge smiles on their faces. Then they walked quickly to Kim and her daughters.

After all the hugging was over, Kim spoke. "We all decided to take a chance and defied my mother and grandmother. We could not allow time to slip by without having the chance to say goodbye. If my father had discovered our plans, we would have been locked away in a guard hut. I am sure of it."

"I am so very glad you and your daughters have come." Turning to Siomara the queen said, "Please fetch Teri from the stables, Siomara. I am sure she would want to say goodbye as well."

Siomara left quickly and found Teri just outside the castle entryway. As they walked in all haste to the sewing room, they heard fairy laughter.

"Are my eyes deceiving me?" Teri shrieked and held out her arms for a group hug. Everyone was talking at once, and Princess Teri tried to answer all the fairies' questions about the after-wedding trip.

Once the chatting died down, Teri turned to Siomara. "Could you fetch the gifts I brought back out of the hallway cupboard, please?" Queen Joyce invited everyone to sit then handed each fairy a tiny fine porcelain teacup. Teri had the pot at the ready and filled the cups with chamomile and honey tea.

At the approach of Siomara, Teri went to her and put the burlap sack on a nearby table, and then spoke. "I found these at a special cottage where a woman set up her shop. She is very popular and her designs are the talk of many places."

Teri nodded, and the queen and Siomara helped her remove the dresses. Handing them one at a time to each fairy, they smiled and were pleased by their reactions. A collective gasp was heard and then giggles, laughter, and chatting voices drifted out into the hallway.

"Teri, these are lovely dresses, but there was no need to purchase a dress for me and two for my mother," Kim said.

"I could not bring all of your daughters a dress without fetching one for you as well, Kim. If it were not for you, I believe I would still be locked in that cage of Agnes's." There was silence, and then the laughter of women and fairies drifted once again throughout the castle.

"Speaking of Agnes, how is she doing?" Kim asked.

Queen Joyce smiled. "She has been keeping the company of Sir Jahaziel quite a lot these days, and I believe in some small way she is helping him through this separation."

Kim raised an eyebrow and stammered, "Really?"

Clearing the many thoughts coming to her mind, Kim turned to the small window to take a cleansing breath, and she quickly placed a hand over her heart. There on a small table near the window sat Patience. She was holding her shaking leaves out for Kim to lift her. "Patience!" she squealed.

Kim grabbed her walking plant and hugged her tight, then spoke. "I see you have done well here living with the queen."

Patients shook her leaves in agreement with Kim's statement. Then the queen spoke with sincerity. "She cannot stay here, Kim. Now that we are drifting apart, I fear she will wither away from sorrow. You must take her home with you."

Queen Joyce took a long leaf gently into her hand and kissed it then said, "Thank you for your friendship, Patience. It was lovely having you as a guest in my home. Be well, little plant, and think of us often." Patience reached out a long leaf to the queen and stroked her cheek.

Orange Fairy became aware that Myles was looking for her, and she made her excuses to the group and quietly disappeared before everyone's sight.

Myles's horse was busy nibbling the sweet grasses in the meeting meadow. Its tail slowly swished back and forth as it swatted at unseen insects, and its slow steps forward ensured the discovery of more delectable grasses.

Myles sat upon the granite rock in the meeting meadow waiting for Orange Fairy to appear. He was not long in his wait, as she sat next to him in one fairy moment. Myles could not help himself as he reached for her and hugged her tightly to him. He let out the breath he did not realize he was holding and spoke.

"I am relieved that we have a few moments to ourselves to be with one another, Orange." He set her aside and looked lovingly into her dark eyes. "I hope I have not gotten you into trouble by asking for this meeting."

"I would not care if I did, Myles. I could not allow you to leave without seeing you first. I want you to know that my sisters and I are all very distressed over this separation, but Renewal has assured me that we still remain bonded regardless of the distance between us."

Myles reached into his inside jacket pocket and retrieved a large piece of rolled canvas. Handing it to Orange Fairy, he said, "This is a gift for you and your family."

Orange Fairy looked surprised and slowly unrolled the canvas. There before her was a well-done painting of Myles and Princess Teri smiling as they held one another with their faces touching and the obvious love that they had for one another showing on their faces.

"We had this portrait done while we were on our after-wedding journey and were going to present it to the king and queen, but Teri decided that I should give it to you, Orange."

When her tears began to flow down her face, Myles gently held her for the last time.

# Chapter Twenty

Jahaziel, Myles, Christopher, King Crawford, and King William traveled back to the trading post/food stop close to the border. Inside they secured a table, wine, bread, cheese, and a few pieces of fruit. They were all leaning down and looking at the map Jahaziel had drawn for them.

"You say you own all this land here, Jahaziel?" William pointed.

"Yes, and I have just acquired my uncle's land and home just beyond the little river. I recently received a letter from my uncle, Sabastian, informing me about his need to move to a smaller home. He handed over his larger home and all its property to Siomara and me freely. I believe we will all have plenty of room and land. We can start rebuilding once we settle our minds on who will live where. There is an inn that borders my land and a few empty cottages inside my property line. Everyone will have a place to stay until we are finished with all the building." Jahaziel straightened up and remained standing.

"You cannot give this land to us, Jahaziel. We will pay a fair price for it and pay for the servant's land as well," Crawford announced.

"I do not want your money. What am I going to do with all this land anyway? It is just open land that I cannot take care of by myself. Siomara has allergies to physical labor and would not think of removing grass, helping with the horses, fixing wagons, or hauling water," Jahaziel finished, and then burst out laughing.

"We get it, Jahaziel. You can stop your litany of Siomara's faults."

"We have each other to lean on and plenty of help when the need arises. I, for one, am glad that it is not such a long journey. It could be worse you know. I could have secured land at the farthest southern coastal region that I was told was up for auction. It would take us a good six months to get there and get settled."

Everyone nodded in agreement, and they signed the contracts that Jahaziel brought with him. He did not want to get into any disputes with other land seekers.

"I have the servant's contracts with me as well. They can all sign them when we return."

Jahaziel sat back down and finished his bread and cheese.

"I understand the servant brothers of Polnairs Retreat have already moved into the abandoned castle in the east. I was told by Servant Bartholomew that you worked well into the night to have it ready for them, Christopher. Was the rebuild difficult?" Crawford asked.

"The supplies I ordered were slow in coming and caused some delays, but I was able to keep my schedule thanks to the Retreat servants. Some of them are quite skilled craftsmen and caught on quickly to my detailed sketches. I left them with a few minor repairs and am settled that they can handle any future difficulties on their own." Turning to King

William, Christopher said, "Oh, I nearly forgot, King William, Servant Bartholomew bid me to tell you to come anytime for retreat when you have need for quiet contemplation."

"I may take Bartholomew up on that after we are all finished with this move." William raised his wine cup to Christopher and began to drink.

"Have you heard anything from Kim, Jahaziel?" Crawford questioned.

"She met me just before we left. Apparently a few fairies, whose names I will not mention, decided to boycott the decision that we were all to leave. They claim to have not been consulted properly and have decided to move to North/Southland with us. When Kim asked them how they were planning on passing as humans, they said they would wear long robes at all times, and if people stared at them, they would inform them that they were midgets and to please have a care for their feelings."

William spit out his wine, and Crawford had to slap his back before he choked and passed out. Myles and Christopher put their heads down on their crossed arms, which rested on the tabletop, and Jahaziel laughed until his sides ached.

Finally, Crawford was able to speak. "None of our women folk seem to be taking this move well, including those fairies you just mentioned, Jahaziel. If I know my wife and daughter, and I do know them very well, they will be crafting lots of gifts and writing too many letters of goodbye at the last minute hoping to delay the inevitable as long as possible. It saddens me to see them so distressed. I truly wish this decision to move was up to me, but as we all know, Renewal's decision is final"

Jahaziel did not want to think about Renewal, and he spoke to change the subject back to the topic at hand.

"I think we need to return as quickly as possible. The next shaking is scheduled to take place four days from now, and I would rather be there when it begins." Crawford nodded to everyone and they stood, left money on the table, and exited the trading post/food stop.

"Christopher and I will be a day or two behind you, King Crawford. We need to look for a few more craftsmen and metallurgists, as well as order supplies and materials to start the building. Christopher has a friend he went to school with who is willing to take charge of storing the things as they arrive. They will be safe with him until we return for the last time," Myles finished.

King Crawford nodded and Myles walked beside Christopher as they went about their business.

The last of the remaining items removed from Fitzhuwlyn, Mead, and Gauwain castles were carefully loaded on to a large rowboat. All the decorative mantle stones from the castles hearths and the wooden beams from their entryways were carefully removed and cut into sections for easier loading. The all-important fountain from the gardens at Fitzhuwlyn Castle was dismantled and packed up into three large wooden crates. The boat nearly sank with the weight from the last load, and Jahaziel had little room for himself as he tensely rowed to the larger cargo ship.

On board to lift the heavy items were, King William, King Crawford, Christopher, Myles, and Sir Gauwain, who jumped into the rowboat to help Jahaziel lift the boxes. King William spoke with a quiet voice. He knew Jahaziel's sorrow weighed heavily upon him.

"That is the last of it, Jahaziel. Take your time saying goodbye to everyone. With a full moon on the rise, we can take our time and steer our way back to North/Southland safely."

Jahaziel nodded, lowered himself back down to the rowboat, and headed back to shore. His mind went back to the first loading and his conversation with King Lutherian.

*"We may have less than one month to gather the last of our people and belongings as well as things of importance, Luther, but I, for one, am not looking forward to the end of this task. I know each day that this land drifts farther and farther away from North/Southland adds more time to the journey back. And each trip back and forth will take longer than the last one."*

*He handed over another box to Christopher to load onto the middle rowboat and continued his conversation.*

*"I still cannot wrap my mind around Renewal's decision to separate this land from the other. I understood her words well and her intention that no human will occupy this land again, but doing what she has demanded is a monumental task to say the least. It is not enough time."*

*In a soft tone, the fey king said, "Ah, you will not miss me all that much, Jahaziel. Besides, we are all here to help you with the move."*

*Jahaziel did not smile at Lutherian's statement.*

Suddenly the sound of Kim's voice broke his reverie. As the boat floated ashore, Jahaziel climbed out and went to her.

"I thought I heard your voice, Jahaziel. Were you talking to yourself?" Kim smiled and floated to him. "Jahaziel, please do not do this. Do not look at me with such sorrowful eyes."

"How can you say this to me, Kim? My heart is breaking with the thought that we will never see one another again. Look at me. My hands shake with a fear I have never experienced before."

Kim had told herself she would not cry. Over and over in her head she repeated, *We are bound forever, we cannot be separated by time or death. Again, we are bound forever, we cannot be separated by time or death.* She burst into tears and her sobs could be heard through the entire land of Phenloris. Jahaziel quickly grabbed her and gently held her in his arms. With a soft hand, he ran his fingers through her long blonde hair and rubbed her back. He thanked the heavens that Renewal changed her mind and did not remove their bonding, and then he spoke for the last time what was in his heart.

"I know that we are bound by this singular fairy thing, Kim. I also know we will never stop thinking of one another, but by all the heavens I feel like I am dying."

His last words were barely heard, and he fought to control his emotions. So there they stayed for several long moments in each other's arms. Grasping, it seemed, for time to stop.

When Kim could no longer take the pain of separation, she disappeared from Jahaziel's embrace.

He knew she would do that, leave him quickly. In that fleeting moment in time he had held the most beautiful creature he would ever lay his eyes upon. Now she was but a memory. Jahaziel wiped his hands through his hair in an effort to comfort himself. The emptiness began to seep into his very soul, and he turned to board the rowboat for the last time.

The sound of Lutherian clearing his throat had him turning back around. Hovering next to him was the entire Clan of Phenloris with the exception of Kim and behind them stood Alywn of Heartmorland.

Lutherian floated forward and spoke with great sincerity, and Jahaziel was deeply moved by their show of support, love, and friendship.

"Jahaziel, we have all decided to bid you farewell, and we are sad to say that we cannot give you a gift to remember us by. However, we all know these were the wishes of Renewal. Nothing of fairies or elves shall be looked upon as proof of our existence. This is the best we could do. Little comfort, I know, but we wish you well in your life and bid you health, happiness, and good fortune. It has been an honor to know you, Sir Jahaziel."

In a splendid show of respect, every fairy and fey lowered themselves to the ground and bowed in homage to the knight. Alwyn lowered his head and joined the creatures of Phenloris in their salutation.

Every word Jahaziel spoke was painful, but he wanted Lutherian to know his strength was present. Now to this land of fairies, feys, strange creatures, and land mermaid, walking plants, guinea pigs, and elves he would leave a piece of his heart. He cleared his throat and reached into his coat pocket.

"Luther, I nearly forgot. Would you please give these letters to those whose names are written upon them?"

Lutherian took the pile and turned over the first letter addressed to him. "King Crawford and King William have pressed their seals upon the folded parchments in red wax as a small memento. You can steam them open without the worry of damaging the seals or letters. Just know they are written from the heart."

Lutherian nodded and began sifting through the letters and was not surprised to see several letters addressed to Kim.

Looking at the clan for the last time, Jahaziel slowly scanned the group. He was determined to memorize every face and every smile. In that last moment, Jahaziel vowed to burn the image of this wondrous clan into his memory. He bowed to them. It was a long, deep respectful bow, and then he straightened, nodded, and boarded the rowboat.

With his back to the bow, Jahaziel faced the shoreline of the unique land he once called home. As he rowed his way to the cargo ship, he could hear the sound of singing in the distance. Jahaziel could not help but smile as one floating torch after another lit themselves, and they gently swayed back and forth of their own accord to the sound of fairy songs.

The full moon reflected its image upon the water, and it seemed to dance in salutation to Jahaziel with each rippling wave from the motion of the oars. Unashamed, Jahaziel let his tears fall freely down his face.

Glenlillian found Kim at the moors of the original land where upon the Clan of Phenloris first settled. It was there that Kim had discovered a very ill Egwin long ago. It was there where she could find peace and comfort. Today the comfort, the peace eluded her, and she ignored the tears that blurred her sight and fell freely down her face.

Glenlillian slowly flitted to Kim and sat down on the bolder next to her daughter. Kim turned to her mother and saw the letters she held tightly to her chest. "These letters are addressed to you, and I have no doubt every single one is written with love, Kim. You, my dear, are a very popular fairy. No one else in this clan has received so many letters. There are seven, here, and I am sure one of them is from Jahaziel," Glenlillian whispered.

"Mother, please. I cannot read them just yet. I cannot."

Glenlillian held her daughter, stroked her hair, and wiped her tears. They were small comforts, she knew, but what else could she do to help Kim through the separation?

Glenlillian looked up at the approach of Huw and quietly gave up her seat on the bolder. Huw took her place and wrapped his arms around Kim. He said nothing to his promised sweet, for he could not find adequate words to comfort such a sorrow.

Egwin was there, just beyond the encampment where Kim nursed him back to health so many years ago. He looked up the hill and at the pair holding on to one another. He could hear Kim crying, and his heart felt heavy. Kim's sorrow and his mingled in his body and this was the first time he wished they had not bonded those years ago.

Alwyn sat upon the stallion King William called Arabian. It was a gift from the king, and he was in awe of the horse. Never had he seen such a breed. As he gently led it down a path toward Newery, Alwyn read the letter from William.

*Alwyn,*

*I am at a loss for words on the final decision from Renewal concerning our exile. The exodus of humans from your lands was difficult for all involved. However, I will not waste good parchment listing the reasons we should have stayed. I will not go there or berate Renewal in any way.*

*Let me just say it has been my pleasure to have known you and a great honor to call you my friend. In our searchings for your father Darrius's executioner, I have come to think of you as family.*

*I married when I was young, and my wife died many years ago giving birth to a stillborn son. I have not been as close to my cousin Queen Joyce as I ought. I have learned a great many things from our talks and the most important advice I have taken from you is the importance of family. No matter how estranged we may find ourselves, family should always be our focus.*

*You are family, Alwyn. Therefore, I have written your name next to my infant son's in my family ledger. It is a human practice often used to keep track of all the children born into royal families. It is an honor for me to see your name written as tangible proof that you exist. Be assured that there are no clues entered about who or where you are.*

*I believe the Arabian stallions will do well in your lands. Three others of its kind, one male and two females, have been presented to your cousin Linden with instructions to give the other two to Egwin and Farian. They are not related in anyway and can be used as breeding pairs.*

*Please tell Elaine and Enos that I have enjoyed their company and intellectual bantering. I am forever grateful that I was able to come to their aid. Old Maggie still seeks them when we are out and about searching fields for oat and wheat, and I have to get use to the idea that she does not understand me and cannot talk back.*

*I fear people find me to be a little queer or insane when hearing me speaking to the horse.*

*I bid you good fortune, my friend.*

*William*

Alwyn placed the letter back into the carrying pouch draped over the stallion he would name William. He burst into laughter thinking what insulting things William would say if he knew he had named the stallion after him.

His smile faded as he slowed the stallion to a stop on the daisy-laden path close to his home. He raised his eyes upward and thanked the heavens King William was with him when Renewal informed him that Mawrthlyn was the one responsible for his father's death. It had taken all of William's strength to hold him back from striking out at Renewal. However, it was her sorrowful demeanor and sincere speech that calmed him enough to accept her final decision concerning Mawrthlyn: crystal encasement. She explained the medicines given him had not helped as she had hoped and crystal encasement was her only recourse concerning Mawrthlyn. So there he would remain encased forever.

Alwyn nudged his horse forward, and they headed for home.

# Epilogue

Jahaziel sat on his favorite chair and scooted himself close to the well-worn table built by Christopher many years ago. He sipped at his now-cooling cup of tea and looked around with appreciation at his surroundings. Bringing the table and chair out-of-doors into the center of the meadow was just what he needed to recover from the recent cold and onslaught of the hordes of grandchildren still running amuck.

The sun was shining down upon him appreciatively, and with the new spring flowers in full bloom, their mingling scents drifted around him. He had purchased the rather large piece of land long ago with the intention of building several homes and buildings for businesses within view of the grand meadow. It was a lovely place for him to retire when the lack of agility and age caught up with him.

Siomara and Gauwain still lived in their uncle Sabastian's house, just steps away over the small walking bridge where the widest part of a winding creek gurgled with splendid sounds. It rushed on beyond his land and continued on through the outlining border of the Fitzhuwlyn's lands. Within their borders, Christopher and Sara had settled so they would be close to all the Fitzhuwlyns. As their children grew, they intermingled with Fitzhuwlyn children, traveled together, and married.

His eldest son, Markus, now occupied Jahaziel's parent's home. Jahaziel had kept up with the family home and property before he and his wife made the final move to North/Southland. They lived there for several years until the newer, larger home was built just a few yards from his parents' house. Looking at the old house brought happy and sad memories to Jahaziel, and his mind recalled the emptiness he felt when he returned to the house for the first time after his parents' deaths.

*They were merchants from North/Southland. On occasion they would bring goods and cloth to King Edward's wife, Queen Lenore, at Allenwood Castle beyond the border near the Aredoe River. It was on a special trip that the queen came to their mercantile to collect a rather large array of cloth, goods, and a newly built wagon crafted by a much sought after artisan. Much to their surprise, Queen Lenore invited Jahaziel's parents to travel back with her to Allenwood knowing they would love to visit their newly knighted and only son.*

*Whether it was insight or fate that his mother left his young sister with family, Jahaziel could not say. He was, however, grateful that the fates had spared Siomara. Upon their return, the river, Aredoe, had overflowed after a great storm, and the sheer force of the water had swept nearly everyone, including horses and wagons, into the sea. Jahaziel recalled Princess Joyce's eighteenth birthday was to be celebrated upon her mother's return. Instead, the king prepared for the funeral of his beautiful queen.*

*Naturally their parents' tragic drowning came as a shock to Jahaziel and his sister, Siomara. King Edward had grown fond of Jahaziel and could not bear to see him return to his home, so he sent for his young sister when the roads were again safe for travel. They made their home in the upper northern valley at Allenwood, and over time both Fitzwhuwlyn and Allenwood were considered home.*

*Many years later, the move back to North/Southland had taken several days, and Jahaziel recalled it was not long after everyone had settled into their own homes that an illness struck suddenly at the heart of the land. They offered their home to the sick and infirmed. Before the illness finished its insidious rampage, it had taken the lives of many of the villagers near and to the east of North/Southland. Yet he believed he and his wife were spared by an invisible hand or magic.*

His mind focused back to the here and now, and he smiled at Agnes, his wife of many years. She was standing at their kitchen back door waving a rather large wooden spoon in the air and bellowing her threats that, obviously, were not taken seriously.

"I promise I will cut off every one of your fingers and knock you senseless with this spoon if you steal one more cookie before I have finished baking the batch!"

The squeals of laughter from the grandchildren bounced around him, and Jahaziel realized at that moment that he was very content.

His hair was no longer the dark auburn color of his youth but streaked in different shades of gray. He had a slight limp from battles won and lost for his king, and his friendship with all of the Fitzhuwlyn's and King William had never wavered in these many years.

It was in quiet moments like this one when his mind was not occupied with the challenges of life in all its diversities that Jahaziel would reflect on a sorrow that never left him. Absently rubbing at his heart, he thanked the heavens and beyond that he could still bring memories of her face to him, her laughter and breathtaking smile, her stubbornness and mischief making, and her love for him and his for her.

Stories about fairies were no longer stated as fact but told to children as fables before tucking them in to bed at night. They were stories told for bold entertainment to win prizes or goods, but stories they were.

There in the quietness of the late afternoon, Jahaziel decided to take Agnes's advice. Reaching down, he lifted the large handcrafted wooden box and placed it on the table. He opened the box and one at a time removed the items contained therein. The blank stack of paper was bound together with one long blue ribbon woven through holes placed evenly at the binding and tied in the center. Immediately it began flipping itself open and close with the help of a playful warm breeze. The five sharpened quills with their lavish feathers purloined from a reluctant pet peacock named Gus made Jahaziel smile at the memory of the grandchildren running after—then running away—from Gus in triumph as they paraded around the house with one feather in each of their hands.

The small dark-blue glass of the corked ink bottle filled nearly to the top with a special blend of ink sparkled like a blue sapphire as the dancing sun played with swiftly moving white clouds. The last item was a rolled parchment tied with a white ribbon. Jahaziel slid the ribbon off, unrolled the map, and scanned it. Satisfied it was complete, he rolled it back up, slid the ribbon in place, and returned it to the box.

With a slight shaking of his right hand, Jahaziel removed the cork from the ink bottle, picked up one of the sharpened quills, gently dipped it into the ink, and tapped it on the bottle's lip. Then he slowly began to write on the second page in lovely script.

*Long ago, in a land no longer remembered, lived a clan of fairies well hidden from men and kings. Their peaceful existence went undisturbed and unnoticed until...*

Jahaziel paused a moment in thought. When the shadow of a large bird crossed over the table, he looked up just as the eagle began its descent. He lifted his left arm, and the eagle landed softly upon it. Jahaziel smiled, raised his right hand palm up, and the eagle dropped his ring into it.

In a soft whisper he spoke, "Tell me where she is old friend."

The eagle jumped onto the table, and Jahaziel put his ring on the little finger of his left hand once again. When he felt a soft breeze at his right ear, he smiled brightly and turned his head. There she stood at the edge of his table with her hands on her hips and a smile so bright upon her face, the sun paled in comparison. Their booming laughter bounced out into the meadow as he asked, "Where have you been, you daft fairy?"

# The End

DON'T FORGET TO PURCHASE YOUR COPY OF THE FAIRY CLAN OF PHENLORIS: AN ADVENTURE IN A MAGICAL LAND BY THERESE GRANT.

# About Therese Grant

herese Grant spent her childhood and teen years in Cleveland, Ohio where she enjoyed the company of her large family. Included in this wonderful menagerie of family were many aunts, uncles, and hordes of cousins. As large families often did in those days, they would gather at one house or another to cook, eat, drink, celebrate, and tell outrageous stories.

Often, when the children gathered together in attics, basements, or out-of-doors, a contest would begin, and a winner was declared after the most outlandishly frightening stories were told. The happy screams of children could be heard echoing up and down the stairs, long hallways, and into the streets.

This began Therese's introduction into the art of fantasy storytelling. Shy by nature, it would take her several years before she would brave an audience. Always losing to a better storyteller, she nevertheless persevered, and never gave up on the idea of creating a great story.

***The Fairy Clan of Phenloris: The Portents of Doom*** is Therese's second work; her first work, ***The Fairy Clan of Phenloris: An Adventure in a Magical Land*** was published in 2013. Receiving much acclaim, it established her place in the literary market as a recognized, professional author.

Therese resides in Columbia, South Carolina with her husband and family. She is constantly surrounded by many of her loveable pets.

234

CPSIA information can be obtained at www.ICGtesting.com
Printed in the USA
LVOW08s0604300616

494705LV00001B/7/P